Dear Reader,

Welcome back to Bachelor Arms! Bachelor number two is a hero near and dear to my heart—*The Strong Silent Type*. You know the kind. They don't say much, but when they do, you can't help but listen. Josh Banks was a great character to write. After all, a tax accountant isn't your typical romance hero. Turning this shy guy into a white knight was a lot of fun. And paired with a wild thing, Josh became the kind of man any woman could love.

Taryn Wilde has a little bit of me inside of her. I've always been a creative person, involved in opera and theater. I've even dabbled in painting and sculpture. But I've never, ever been as outrageous as this heroine. Since there aren't too many jet-set party girls living in my quiet neighborhood in Milwaukee, Wisconsin, I'll just have to live vicariously through Taryn.

Next month will wrap up my time at Bachelor Arms. In *A Happily Unmarried Man*, bachelor Garrett McCabe will meet his match. I love to hear from my readers. You can write to me in care of Harlequin Books.

Sincerely,

Kate Hoffmann

c/o Harlequin Temptation
225 Duncan Mill Road
Don Mills, Ontario M3B 3K9
Canada

**BACHELOR
ARMS**

Come live and love in L.A. with the tenants of Bachelor Arms

Bachelor Arms is a trendy apartment building with some very colorful tenants. Meet three confirmed bachelors who are determined to stay single until three very special women turn their lives upside down; college friends who reunite to plan a wedding; a cynical and sexy lawyer; a director who's renowned for his hedonistic life-style, and many more…including one very mysterious and legendary tenant. And while everyone tries to ignore the legend, every once in a while something strange happens.…

Each of these fascinating people has a tale of success or failure, love or heartbreak. But their stories don't stay a secret for long in the hallways of Bachelor Arms.

Bachelor Arms is a captivating place, home to an eclectic group of neighbors. All of them have one thing in common, though—the feeling of community that is very much a part of living at Bachelor Arms.

BACHELOR ARMS

THE TENANTS OF BACHELOR ARMS

Ken Amberson: The odd superintendent who knows more than he admits about the legend of Bachelor Arms.

Josh Banks: The strong, silent type. A financial whiz who is more comfortable with numbers than with women.

Eddie Cassidy: Local bartender at Flynn's next door. He's looking for his big break as a screenwriter.

Jill Foyle: This sexy, recently divorced interior designer moved to L.A. to begin a new life.

Tru Hallihan: A loner P.I. who loves 'em and leaves 'em.

Natasha Kuryan: This elderly Russian-born femme fatale was a makeup artist to the stars of yesterday.

Garrett McCabe: A confirmed bachelor whose newspaper column touts the advantages of single life.

Brenda Muir: Young, enthusiastic would-be actress who supports herself as a waitress.

Bobbie-Sue O'Hara: Brenda's best friend. She works as an actress and waitress but knows that real power lies on the other side of the camera.

Bob Robinson: This barfly seems to live at Flynn's and has an opinion about everyone and everything.

Theodore "Teddy" Smith: The resident Lothario—any new female in the building puts a sparkle in his eye.

THE STRONG SILENT TYPE

KATE HOFFMANN

Harlequin Books

TORONTO • NEW YORK • LONDON
AMSTERDAM • PARIS • SYDNEY • HAMBURG
STOCKHOLM • ATHENS • TOKYO • MILAN
MADRID • WARSAW • BUDAPEST • AUCKLAND

ISBN 0-373-25629-9

THE STRONG SILENT TYPE

Copyright © 1995 by Peggy Hoffmann.

1

TARYN LA TERRIBILE!

Though Josh Banks didn't read Italian, it wasn't hard to translate the headline on the glossy front page of the two-month-old copy of *Ieri*, Italy's answer to the supermarket tabloid.

Taryn the Terrible.

He glanced down at the photo that accompanied the clamorous headline. He'd seen her picture once before, on her grandmother's mantel, a picture taken when she was still a gawky teenager of fifteen or sixteen. He recalled wide eyes and hollow cheeks, mousy brown hair and a mouth full of orthodontic apparatus. And he remembered feeling pity for the homely young girl who had been left an orphan at age nine.

But Taryn Wilde was no longer a teenager. In the twelve years since that school photo had been taken, she had grown into a beautiful woman. Her hair was now blond and her teeth perfectly straight. But her face still held that waiflike innocence that belied the scene caught by the paparazzi.

There she was. Taryn the Terrible being restrained by a policeman—his arms wrapped around her waist and her feet off the ground—while she struck another officer on the head with a large and rather deadly-looking designer handbag. The black-and-white image revealed a great deal of leg and a tantalizing glimpse of breast. As he studied the photo more closely, he was stunned to realize that all she wore was a black tuxedo jacket, bikini underwear, a long string of pearls, and high heels. The photographer had snapped the shutter the moment before her enormous purse struck its target. The surrounding crowd was captured in an array of shocked and delighted expressions.

He was drawn again to that face, the tiny nose, the mouth that seemed permanently upturned at the corners, the wide, luminous eyes. Though he couldn't determine the color, he could tell they were pale, very pale and very unforgettable. He found it hard to believe that someone with such a perfectly sweet and innocent appearance would assault an officer of the law. His gaze skimmed back over the photo.

"She is out of control, I tell you!"

Olivia Wilde's voice echoed through the staid silence of Josh's office, startling him out of his idle contemplation of Taryn Wilde's right thigh. Two spots of color rose in Olivia Wilde's pale, parchment cheeks and her breath came in fast, uneven gasps. Josh dropped the newspaper and quickly grabbed the pitcher of water on his desk. When he'd sloshed enough into a glass, he held it out to her. "Here," he ordered. "Drink this." She snatched it from his hand and gave him an annoyed glare.

"Don't worry, young man. I'm not about to keel over in your office. I may be old but I still know how to make a masterful exit. Dropping dead in my business manager's office would be dreadfully mundane. When I go, I'm going to go with style."

Olivia sipped at the water. To Josh's great relief, her color and her breathing returned to normal. He watched her carefully, ready to jump up and assist in an emergency. After all, she was nearly seventy-five years old and he didn't want her keeling over in his office any more than she did. "I certainly hope you're not planning to leave this world soon, Miss Wilde," he commented. "You have some municipal bonds coming due in three months and there will be enough profit to build that greenhouse you've been wanting."

Olivia laughed. Though Josh could detect nothing humorous in his statement, Olivia always seemed to find a great deal of amusement in his serious and forthright comments. Strange that his five sisters and his mother still insisted he had no sense of humor. If Olivia found him funny, maybe he was finally developing one.

The fact was, he preferred to approach life in the same way he did his clients' finances—in a very cautious manner, always evaluating and studying, weighing the risk against the opportunity for success. And though most would call him conservative, he preferred to think of himself as conscientious and practical—qualities that seemed to complement his innate reticence.

"Is that supposed to be a bribe?" she teased.

Josh frowned. "No, it's a statement of fact. At twelve percent, the bonds should give us an outstanding return. I've penciled the greenhouse into next quarter's home improvement budget."

"What would I do without my clever young man?" she asked fondly. "When I came to you, I was nearly broke. My career was over, my life was in a shambles. I thought I'd end up in one of those homes where old movie stars go to die. Then you took the tiny bit of money I had left and saved my life. I owe you so much, Josh."

Josh distractedly pushed his wire-rimmed glasses up the bridge of his nose and fought back a surge of self-consciousness. He'd never learned to accept a compliment, especially one from a client. He was simply doing his job, doing what he got paid for. And if he managed to save money or make money for them, then that was that.

They acted as if what he did were as complex and significant as brain surgery. Although in Hollywood terms, a good tax accountant probably was worth three or four competent brain surgeons.

"I owe you a great deal, too, Miss Wilde," he murmured. "You were my first client." He recalled the day Olivia Wilde appeared in his tiny Hollywood office eight years ago. He had seen many of her old movies and recognized her immediately. She'd worked with all the great leading men of the forties and fifties—Humphrey Bogart, Gregory Peck, Cary Grant. But as she grew older, the parts had come fewer and far between. On the day they met, Olivia hadn't worked in nearly twelve years. Her savings were nearly gone and she was desperate—desperate enough to hire a fledgling tax accountant to manage her money.

In less than a year, he had her financial problems turned around. Along the way, he had picked up the business affairs of some of Olivia's old Hollywood friends, friends whose stars—and financial resources—had faded, much like hers.

They'd both come a long way since the day they'd met. The office in Hollywood had been replaced with a luxurious office suite in Beverly Hills and a staff of twenty. He now managed all of Olivia's tidy little nest egg, along with the taxes of some of the most powerful people in Hollywood. He had much wealthier clients than Olivia Wilde, but it made no difference—she was his first and favorite. He had vowed long ago that he would take care of Olivia until she left this life. He owed her that much and more.

Now, in the twilight of her career, she had taken a small role in a low-budget feature that the critics had lauded and the public had adored. At age seventy-five, Olivia Wilde was touted as the front-runner for a Best Supporting Actress Oscar. The Academy Award nomination ballots would be mailed next week and the stress was starting to show in his favorite client.

"She's back you know," Olivia stated.

"Your granddaughter has returned to the States?" Josh asked.

"Taryn's been in Los Angeles for nearly a month. And already she's causing a stir." Olivia dug through her handbag and pulled out a newspaper clipping, then handed it to Josh. "Of course, the tabloids are thrilled she's returned from Italy. Before you know it, she'll replace that singer...." Olivia waved her hand dramatically. "You know, the one who wears those naughty costumes. Taryn will replace *her* as the tabloids' darling, mark my words."

"Why did she come home?" Josh asked.

Olivia shook her head, her perfectly coiffed gray hair as stiff as her unsmiling mouth. "I don't know," she replied. "Maybe they kicked her out of the country. She's no longer with that Hungarian baron or prince or whatever he was."

"I believe he was Italian," Josh said, recalling another newspaper clipping Olivia had shown him. "And as I recall, he was a count."

"Whatever. My granddaughter has picked the worst time in the world to return to the States. She could ruin my last chance for an Oscar."

"How could she do that, Miss Wilde? Your performance speaks for itself and that's what's being judged, isn't it?"

"You're so innocent to the ways of Hollywood, dear boy. My performance is only part of it. Do you remember Diana Darling?"

Josh frowned. "No. Who was she?"

"She was the so-called shoo-in for a Best Actress award in 1953. Until her husband got involved in a messy affair with a nightclub dancer. And then there's Harmon Cummings and that little problem with his taxes. And Jocelyn Stewart and her penchant for handsome younger men. All of them had an award well within their grasp until some scandal snatched it away. And now, no one even remembers their names."

"Have you talked to Taryn? Maybe if you told her what's at stake, she'd agree to keep a low profile."

"Josh, my granddaughter and I are barely on speaking terms. We hardly know each other. After my son, Oliver, and Taryn's mother died in that awful car crash nearly twenty years ago, she came to live with me for a time. I was named her guardian, but I knew nothing about raising a child. I had hired a nanny to raise Oliver and you know how badly he turned out. Not that my son and that wife of his did any better by Taryn. Oliver was absorbed in his own rather notorious film career and his wife was absorbed in herself. When Taryn came to live with me, I was busy trying to keep my career afloat, and I had no time for her. So I put her in a boarding school out east and later, when she started to rebel, I shipped her off to a school in Switzerland."

"What does she do to support herself?" Josh asked.

"Whatever whim strikes her at the moment. She's done some modeling, she's had some success as a painter and a sculptress, she sang in a ridiculous rock band, she's designed haute couture, she's even done some acting. Most recently she's been involved in—in performance art. According to that tabloid, she was arrested after she—" the pink spots returned to her wrinkled cheeks "—she removed her clothes during one of her performances." Olivia sighed. "She's what we used to call bohemian, a free spirit. But in this day and age we simply call it irresponsible."

"And that's how she makes a living?" Josh asked. "By removing her clothes?"

"Oh, it's not lurid and sleazy like those girls on Hollywood Boulevard," Olivia assured him. "It's art. They have naked statues in public squares and museums all over Italy. It's not like they don't see it every day. I can't imagine why they arrested her."

"Why do you think she's returned?"

"I'm not sure, but I have a feeling she might need money. She received a generous trust fund from her parents' estate when she turned twenty-one, but with the way she's lived, there probably isn't much left."

"So, you'd like me to manage her money?" Josh asked.

"No, silly boy," Olivia replied dryly. "I'd like you to kidnap her and lock her up until after the Oscar votes are in."

Josh frowned. "I believe that would be against the law, Miss Wilde."

Olivia chuckled and waved the lace handkerchief she held, her swift change of mood confusing Josh. "You do have a way of making me feel better, Josh. Your dry wit is just the thing for my black mood."

His dry wit? He wasn't *trying* to be funny. There was nothing humorous about conspiracy to commit a federal offense. Kidnapping was against the law and he'd never agree to be part of such a plan. Surely, Olivia Wilde understood that. Besides, it had taken *two* Italian police officers to apprehend Taryn Wilde after her performance. Kidnapping her on his own would probably be impossible.

"All right, if you won't agree to kidnapping, I'd like you to find her and talk to her," Olivia continued. "Explain what's at stake. Tell her how important this is to me."

"Certainly she must know. After all the bad times you went through, nearly losing everything, she must—"

"She knows nothing about that time. As far as she's concerned, I've always been well-off. I maintained an image, for both Taryn and my public, and it cost me dearly."

"And I'm sure her education cost you dearly, too. She should know what you sacrificed."

Olivia wagged her finger at him. "I've never cared for the role of the long suffering martyr, my dear. I was always more inclined toward the lighter, comedic heroine. And you will not tell her, is that understood?"

With that, Olivia stood and brushed the wrinkles from the skirt of her tailored suit. She was a tall, slender woman, almost imperial in her appearance and demeanor with steel gray hair and piercing eyes—definitely a woman to be reckoned with. "I want you to find her and talk to her. I have no idea where she's staying, but as I said, you're a clever boy. I'm sure you can track her down. You have my permission to offer her money to leave the country for a few months. Buy her a plane ticket back to Venice or Paris or Siberia—wherever she came from, just send her back there. I want her away from Los Angeles and out of the view of the media and the Academy members until the final votes are in."

Josh stood, holding out his hands in a gesture of reluctance. "Miss Wilde, this really isn't something I should be—"

"You are the only one I can trust with this," she replied. "*You* are in charge of my financial future, Josh, and an Academy Award could make that future much more comfortable." She smiled. "So, you see, in a way, this *is* your responsibility, dear boy. Now, I must go. I have a luncheon appointment with an old friend. Ronnie and I haven't seen each other since before he left for the White House." She walked to the door, then turned back to him. "You'll let me know how it all goes, won't you?"

He rushed to the door and pulled it open for her. "Of course, Miss Wilde," he murmured.

She smiled and placed her palm on his cheek. "You really are a dear, Josh. I don't know what I'd do without you." She waved as she walked through the reception area and out of the office.

Josh stared after her. When he heard the front office door close, he wandered back to his desk, then released a pent-up breath and flopped back into his chair. He'd never learned to say no, especially to Olivia. And he owed her this, even if he wasn't entirely comfortable playing babysitter to Taryn the Terrible.

His gaze returned to the tabloid and its front-page photo. In a way, he felt badly for Taryn. Josh knew the pain of losing a parent. His father had died of a heart attack when Josh was twelve. In a sense, he too had been left alone. But never completely, as the only male in a houseful of six females. Yet even though he and Taryn shared that same childhood scar, their lives had taken divergent paths from that point.

Josh had been surrounded by a loving family: his mother, three older and two younger sisters. After losing his father, he had dealt with his pain by retreating into a private world where he could cope with the pressures of being the "man" of the family, his mother and sisters fussing over him like a flock of hens.

But Taryn had seen the opposite side of his coin. No one had had time for her as a child. She had been shuffled into the background while her grandmother and father stood in the spotlight of celebrity. He could imagine Taryn as a little girl, hoping, praying that for one moment, the light might shine on her and she'd be noticed. And then to lose everything—her father and mother, her childhood, all that was familiar to her—in one fiery car crash on a winding mountain road in France.

She was certainly noticed now. The public couldn't seem to get enough of her as an adult. Her famous grandmother and infamous father had left a colorful legacy that the press and the public seemed endlessly intrigued by. The small number of movies her father had made before his death were now considered classics. He'd become almost a cult figure in Europe, a prince of the silver screen, and she was the closest thing to American royalty. Even he had been a bit fascinated by the stories of her escapades across Europe.

Josh frowned and tossed the paper on his desk. He had a undergraduate degree in tax accounting from Northwestern and an M.B.A. from Princeton. He knew every tax law and loophole by heart. He knew deductions and depreciation, tax-sheltered annuities and straight-line amortization. But as he gazed down at the photo, unable to drag his eyes away from her face, he realized that he knew absolutely nothing about women.

Especially a woman as beautiful and free-spirited as Taryn Wilde.

"ARE YOU SURE this is where she lives?" Josh looked up at the old, redbrick warehouse, then over at his friend, Tru Hallihan. He had asked Tru, a private investigator and a good friend, to help him locate Taryn Wilde. It had taken Tru less than a day to track Taryn to an older section of Hollywood.

"This is it," Tru replied. "This kind of space is really big with artistic types. Old theaters, sound stages. They've taken a lot of these abandoned buildings and turned them into artists' lofts. Very trendy, very spacious. And it used to be a pretty cheap way to live in L.A., until the wanna-bes discovered how nice these places could be and the values skyrocketed. This building used to house a set workshop for one of the movie studios. The loft is owned by a Margaux Fortier. She runs the Talbot Gallery on La Cienega Boulevard."

"Why would anyone want to live in an old warehouse?"

"Same reason you still live in Bachelor Arms," Tru said.

"How can you compare Bachelor Arms with this? You live there. Garrett lives there. It's much nicer than this."

"I live there because, at one time, it was all I could afford. Garrett lives there because he's afraid that the minute he moves, he'll get a job offer in another city and he'll have to move again. And I've never quite figured out why you still live there."

"What do you mean?" Josh asked.

"Josh, you've got the money to buy a nice house in any number of expensive neighborhoods."

"I like my apartment," Josh explained. "It's practical, it's comfortable, it's convenient, and it's inexpensive. Why would I want to invest all that time and money in a house when I don't need that much room?"

"Because you can afford it," Tru said.

Josh evaluated Tru's statement. He was right. He could afford a more luxurious place. He could afford a lot of things. "I can afford it because I don't waste my money on things I really don't need, like a fancy house or an expensive sports car."

Tru shook his head. "You drive a Volvo sedan, Josh. It's not the most exciting car."

"It's economical and very, very safe."

"With all the money you've taken off of us at Tuesday night poker, you could buy yourself a Ferrari or a even a Maserati, something flashier."

He and Tru and Garrett McCabe, all tenants of the Bachelor Arms apartment building, had a standing poker game at Flynn's, the bar next door to Bachelor Arms, every Tuesday night. The trio had met over a year ago in the basement laundry room at the Arms. After three consecutive Tuesday nights in the basement, they all had decided to make better use of the time with a poker game at Flynn's. Eddie Cassidy, the regular bartender, and Bob Robinson, the bar's most dedicated patron, also played. "Are we playing next week?" Josh asked.

"Sure," Tru replied. "Why not?"

"Aren't you getting married next Saturday?" Josh asked. Tru was supposed to marry Dr. Caroline Leighton, otherwise known as Dr. Carly Lovelace, L.A.'s most popular radio-talk-show psychologist. They had announced their engagement at Christmas, after a rather unorthodox meeting and courtship. Tru had recently begun a security consulting job with Marshall Enterprises. Caroline was soon to be host of her own syndicated television talk show.

Tru shrugged. "Yeah, but I don't have to get ready *that* early. I figured I'd get dressed that morning."

"Don't you have to move?"

"Most of my stuff is already over at Caroline's," Tru explained. "Besides, Ken Amberson made me sign a year's lease on 1-G. I've got the apartment for another nine months, so I don't need to hurry and pack. Hey, you don't know of anyone who might want to sublet the place, do you?"

"You shouldn't have trouble finding a tenant," Josh replied. "It's a nice apartment with reasonable rent."

"And it even comes with its own resident ghost," Tru said with a laugh.

Josh frowned. A vague memory tugged at the back of his mind and he recalled talk about a ghost . . . and a mirror . . . that day he'd helped Tru move out of his old apartment and into 1-G. He'd seen a strange reflection in the mirror in Tru's apartment that day, a fleeting glimpse of a woman, probably someone passing by in the hall. But certainly Tru couldn't believe the mirror was haunted, could he? Josh brushed the thought from his mind.

He really should learn to pay more attention. But idle conversation usually didn't prove to be of much interest to him and he was easily distracted and often preoccupied with his own thoughts. Besides, he had never been adept at either end of social small talk and preferred to remain the silent observer in most conversations.

"So, are you going to wait here until she comes out, or are you going in?" Tru asked.

Josh kept his eyes fixed on the redbrick building. "What?" he asked vaguely.

"The front door's over there. She's on the third floor. Number 3-B. There's a security keypad, so you can probably get as far as her apartment door without a problem. The code is 7-7-3-7."

"How do you know that?" Josh asked.

"Don't ask," Tru said. He turned and climbed in his car. "Good luck." He started his Caddy and pulled away from the curb, leaving Josh to continue his study of the building.

Finally, after another ten minutes, Josh decided it was time to take care of Taryn the Terrible. It was nearly 10:00 a.m. and he was wasting valuable time avoiding the inevitable. They'd have a calm, rational discussion and after he explained the situation, Olivia's granddaughter would agree to go back to Europe for the next three months. Then he would go back to the office and get some important work done.

He crossed the street and walked toward the front door. Apartment 3-B was listed on the security panel with the name Fortier beside it. He punched in the code and the front door responded with a buzz and click of the lock. He pulled it open and walked inside.

Though work had been done to turn the building into habitable space, it still looked like a warehouse to him. After a brief search, he found an ancient freight elevator. Rather than risk his life, he decided to take the fire stairs. Taryn's front door was made of industrial strength sheet metal with a tiny peephole in the center. He knocked and seconds later the door slid open.

"It's about time you got here," she said. "How did you get in?"

Josh stood rooted in his spot as he watched an inquisitive look cross her face. She looked so much younger than he'd expected. She wore a plain blue sleeveless dress, baggy and unflattering and stained with paint. Her hair was a shade darker than the bleached blond color in the tabloid photo, and her pale eyes were an odd mixture of blue and gray. She wore no makeup, yet her ivory skin appeared flawless. He found himself wondering whether it would feel as soft as it looked.

"The front door," Josh said.

"So, are you going to come in or do you plan to stand out in the hall all morning?"

Josh nodded and stepped through the door. "You were expecting me?" he asked.

Taryn pushed the door closed and nodded. "She called yesterday and told me you'd be coming today." She observed him critically, circling him, her thumb tucked under her chin and her finger stroking her cheek. "You're not exactly what I expected."

"What did you expect?"

"Certainly not a suit and tie," she said, the corners of her mouth curled up in an impish smile.

Josh looked down at his navy blue Brooks Brothers suit and silk tie. "This is what I usually wear to work." She reached out and smoothed her hand down his lapel. At the touch of her delicate hand, his blood warmed. She had lovely fingers, long and tapered.

"It does make a rather facetious little statement about the bourgeois attitude toward art in this country. I like it," Taryn said, patting him on the chest. "Well, we'd best get to it. You can undress behind that screen." She pointed to an ornately painted Oriental piece standing in the corner of a huge, airy room. A large canvas, splashed with bright colors, stood near the screen on an easel, right below a skylight. More paintings were propped against every inch of wall space and rolled canvases were scattered in front of them. "Hurry it up, though. The light's nearly perfect."

"You want me to undress?" Josh asked, baffled.

"You don't expect me to paint you while you're dressed in *that*, do you? All those layers hide the musculature and bone structure. I'm paying for a nude model and I expect you to remove your clothing. All of it."

Josh opened his mouth but he was at a loss for a reply. She thought he was a nude model? He nervously shoved his glasses up the bridge of his nose and glanced around the room, avoiding her perceptive gaze.

Taryn sighed. "Don't tell me this is your first time," she said. "I told Margaux I wanted someone with experience."

"Miss Wilde, I—"

"Good Lord, don't call me, Miss Wilde. My grandmother is *Miss* Wilde. If you're going to get naked in front of me, you might as well call me Taryn. But I'd rather not know your name. I prefer to think of you as Everyman rather than someone with an absolute identity."

"Taryn," he repeated. "I'm afraid I'm not going to . . . to get . . . naked in front of you."

She groaned and shook her head. "Please, don't flatter yourself. This always happens with amateurs."

"Amateurs?"

"You have an idiotic and extremely naive fantasy that as soon as I catch sight of your gorgeous body, I'm going to throw you across the bed and have my way with you. Isn't that right? Well, don't worry, as far as I'm concerned you're just a mass of flesh and bone without any sexual identity. Now, get over there and take your clothes off."

"I may be a mass of flesh and bone, but I'm also your grandmother's accountant," he explained. "My name is Josh Banks."

She blinked, her long, sooty lashes coming to rest on her cheeks for a tantalizing instant. "You're what?"

"I believe you have me confused with someone else. I'm not here to model for your painting, I'm here to discuss your grandmother with you."

"You're not the model Margaux sent?" she asked.

"No."

She gave him the once-over then shrugged. "Pity. It looks like you have a rather nice body beneath that stuffy old suit." She stepped around him and yanked open the door, then stood and watched him, tapping her foot impatiently and waiting for him to make his exit.

He wasn't about to leave. The defiant set to her mouth told him that if he walked out that door now, she'd never let him back in. He was here to achieve one goal and one goal only—to convince Taryn Wilde to leave Los Angeles—and he wouldn't walk out until he'd accomplished just that.

"Either you are incredibly obtuse or you're an ill-mannered cretin. This is the door," she said with a flourish of her hand. "I'm holding it open. That means I'd like you to leave now."

"I'm not going anywhere until we talk," Josh replied. He walked slowly into the room, toward her painting. He'd never understood art, or artists for that matter. They seemed to thrive on spontaneity and turmoil. Her painting looked as if she'd thrown the colors at the canvas in a fit of anger. He couldn't make out a resemblance to anything real. Taryn obviously had a vivid imagination—or a savage temper.

"If my grandmother sent you," she called, "you're wasting your time. She and I don't communicate. We never have."

Josh glanced over his shoulder at her. Her arms were crossed over her breasts and she was rubbing her upper arms. Her stubborn expression had suddenly turned vulnerable. Lord, she had incredible eyes. "Your grandmother has a very good chance of being nominated for an Academy Award. The ballots are about to go out and the nominations will be announced early next month."

"So? What does that have to do with me?" Taryn asked.

"The tabloids seem to take great pleasure in reporting your rather...unconventional behavior. Any negative press could hurt your grandmother's chances for a nomination."

Taryn laughed. "So, she sent you here to tell me to behave?"

Josh turned back to the painting. "Not exactly," he murmured. "She sent me here to ask you to leave town until after the Awards ceremony in early April."

She stepped to his side and looked up at him, brow arched. "Isn't that interesting. What if she doesn't get the nomination?"

A smudge of blue paint on her cheek marred her otherwise perfect complexion. He clenched his hands behind his back and fought the impulse to reach out and wipe it away, to restore perfection. "Then, of course, you can . . . return."

She smiled stiffly. "I don't plan to leave. And I don't plan to alter my life-style to suit my grandmother."

He blinked hard, breaking the spell she'd cast with her mesmerizing gaze. "We'd be willing to compensate you for any of your travel expenses. You can go wherever you'd like. Certainly there must be a place more conducive to your art than Los Angeles."

"I'm here because this is where I want to be. I've been offered a show at the Talbot Gallery in mid-April and I need to get ready for it. So, you see, you've wasted your time. You can tell my grandmother I'm not leaving."

Josh cursed inwardly. This was not going at all as he'd planned. He was doing something wrong, but he hadn't a clue as to what it was. Maybe it would be best to try again another time. Josh started for the door and then decided to make one more attempt. "All right," he conceded. "If you won't leave, would you at least agree to curb your behavior?"

"You've been spending too much time with Olivia," she said with a harsh laugh. "You're beginning to sound just like her."

"Will you agree?"

"Who do you think you are, my keeper?"

"If need be," Josh replied calmly. "I owe your grandmother a great debt and I mean to see it repaid in her lifetime. If you do anything to jeopardize her chance for this award, you'll have to answer to me."

"Is that a threat?" she asked.

"No," Josh said, surprised that she had taken his statement in such a negative way. "I simply want you to understand how much this means to your grandmother."

She regarded him through haughty eyes. "If I say I'll behave, will you leave?"

"Only if you mean what you say," Josh said.

She smiled sweetly. "Well, you'll just have to wait and see, won't you?"

Footsteps sounded behind him in the hallway and he turned and watched as a tall, young man stopped in the doorway. The guy grinned at Josh, then glanced into the apartment and sent Taryn an overly friendly smile. Josh felt a strange mixture of mistrust and protectiveness surge through him.

"Are you Taryn Wilde?" the guy asked.

"Yes!" Taryn cried, crossing the room to link her arm in his. She pulled him into the apartment. "You must be the model Margaux sent."

"I'm Mike—"

She held up her hand to stop his words. "No, no! Don't tell me your name," she warned. "I prefer to think of you as simply a man rather than someone with an absolute identity. You can undress over there."

The model walked to the corner of the room and stepped behind the screen. Josh watched in disbelief as, moments later, a shirt was draped over the top. Mike's jeans soon followed. She was serious about this nudity thing! In a matter of seconds, the guy would step from behind that screen, peeled down to his "flesh and bone."

"Do you plan to stay and watch?" Taryn asked.

His gaze snapped back to hers. "No!" he said, backing out the door. "No. I—I think I'll be going now. You'll remember what we discussed?"

"Oh, I will," she said, slowly sliding the door closed.

His hand shot through the opening and he held out his business card. "Both my office and home number are on this card. If you have any questions or concerns, if you need any money, don't hesitate to call me."

She snatched the card from his fingers. "I won't. Bye-bye, Mr. Banks. Give my best to Olivia."

Josh stood in the hall, staring at the closed door for a long time, wondering just what was going on inside the loft. He could imagine her standing before her easel, dabbing paint on the canvas. He could imagine the light from above, glinting in her hair and bathing her in gold. He could even imagine her smile as she worked, curling the corners of her perfect mouth.

What he didn't want to picture was Taryn Wilde, holed up inside her apartment for hours . . . with a naked man.

TARYN STEPPED AWAY from the door and walked over to her canvas. She stared at the painting in progress for a long moment, then sighed. "What's your name?" she called as she snatched up a dirty brush and distractedly swirled it in a tin can of paint thinner.

"Mike," the model replied. "I thought you didn't want to know my name." He appeared from behind the screen.

She idly cleaned the brush with a rag as she evaluated the man's body. Mike was exactly what she had ordered, in fact he was quite a bit more than she had ordered. An aspiring actor, no doubt, who made his living waiting tables and posing for artists. He was a perfect male specimen, an Adonis, with a beautifully sculpted body and a perfectly balanced face. Exactly what she had thought she wanted—until she'd gotten a look at Josh Banks. "You can put your clothes back on," she said bleakly. "I've lost the mood entirely."

"You're sure?" he asked, bracing his arm on the screen, casually unaware of his state of undress. "I can wait for a while if you'd like."

Taryn shook her head. "No," she said. "I've got too much on my mind to concentrate right now. I'll pay you for your time."

"Margaux already paid me. Will you need me tomorrow?"

"I don't think so. I was really looking for someone a little . . . leaner." *Someone with a body exactly like . . . like Josh Banks.* She groaned inwardly. Of all the creative cesspools she'd ever found herself in, this was the worst. She wanted to paint a bloody accountant! "Not that you don't have a terrific body," Taryn assured him, "but it's just not what I had in mind."

"No problem," Mike said. "I'll let Margaux know and she can send someone else."

A few minutes later, she showed a fully dressed Adonis the door then slid it shut behind him and leaned against the smooth steel. It wasn't only the body, she mused. Though, for an accountant, Josh Banks had an extraordinary physique. Tall, broad-shouldered, with a narrow waist and long, muscular legs. Oddly enough, his conservative suit didn't hide his body, merely enhanced it. His crisp white shirt outlined the contours of his torso, his jacket accented the breadth of his shoulders, and his pleated trousers emphasized his flat abdomen.

But there was something else about Josh Banks that she found strangely compelling, something beyond the physical. An odd mixture of repressed sensuality and cool detachment, both cloaking an undeniable masculinity. A silent strength that seemed to radiate from him like heat from the summer sun. She wanted, no she needed, to expose the man beneath that straitlaced armor and capture his energy on canvas.

The series of male nudes she had planned as the centerpiece of her showing had been an elusive project. She'd started working on them in Italy, but had managed only a few mediocre attempts. No matter where she had tried to find peace, the tabloids had always found her. They had camped outside her rented villa twenty-four hours a day while she had been trapped inside, desperate to work, yet faced with a frustrating creative block. When Margaux had suggested she return to the States to work, Taryn jumped at the chance.

Her life in Europe had nearly become intolerable. Though her rather unconventional lifestyle had seemed so exciting, so satisfying when she was younger, Taryn had found herself increasingly restless of late. The wild parties, the uninhibited behavior, the licentious spending sprees, had all been part of who she was. And that person was fast becoming a stranger.

When had her disenchantment begun? She'd tried, again and again, to pinpoint the moment she had turned her back on her old life and decided to start anew. Maybe it had begun with her increasing boredom with her circle of shallow jet-setting friends—pretty, rich playboys and vain party girls. But when had she realized she was merely an amusement for them all?

To them, she was Taryn Wilde, the last of a legendary Hollywood family that stretched back four generations to her great-grandfather, a silent film star. Her own father had become almost a cult figure in Europe, a rather macabre fact that seemed to make her even more popular with the party crowd and the *paparazzi*. Like an exotic bird in a gilded cage, she felt as if her life had become entertainment for her "friends" and for the masses, watched so carefully with such absurd anticipation and malicious glee.

Maybe the incident with the *polizia* at the nightclub in Rome had been the final straw. Two hours after *Ieri* had hit the newsstands, filled with outrageous lies and that embarrassing photo, Taryn was packing her bags. Two minutes before she walked out of her rented villa, Margaux Fortier had called with news that would change the course of her life.

Margaux had just sold one of Taryn's paintings to a major collector, a collector who wanted to see more of her work. So her friend, smart businesswoman that she was, made an offer—a major gallery showing, a vital step in an artist's career. Taryn had always been told she had talent as an artist, but she'd never really bothered to believe it. Now she had to. After all, Margaux had sold the painting for three thousand dollars.

Taryn drew a deep breath. She needed this focus to her life, an opportunity to build a real future, away from her crazy past. And she felt good about herself when she painted—hopeful, as if someday she might be recognized for more than just her outrageous behavior. She wanted to be worth something long after her trust fund went dry and her jet-setting friends moved on to someone else.

She was never quite sure why she had made the choices she had, why she had chosen such a rebellious, free-spirited path. Her last lover had once blurted his theory out in the midst of an argument. He had speculated that her behavior was merely a way to punish her grandmother, and her dead parents, a silly appeal for the love and attention she had missed as a child. Though she had brushed his theory off with a derisive laugh and swift slap across the face, his words had haunted her nearly every day for the past two years.

In a way, she had come to L.A. to prove him wrong. She didn't need the attention the tabloid press brought her to be happy. Except for one minor photograph in a recent issue of the *Inquisitor*, she had managed to avoid them entirely. And she didn't need anyone's love to feel content or fulfilled. She was fine on her own. And she certainly didn't need her grandmother's approval ' efore she could be satisfied with her life.

Taryn reached out and touched the surface of the painting. What she really needed was Josh Banks. The man was a perfect study in contrasts—icy calm, blazing heat—exactly the concept she was trying to portray in her paintings. If she could get him to pose for her, just maybe she could paint the passion that she knew was hidden behind that unaffected, conservative exterior. Maybe she could capture his quiet sensuality with her brush.

All she had to do now was convince her grandmother's accountant to take his clothes off for her. Her future depended on it.

2

"EXACTLY WHAT *DO* WOMEN DO at a wedding shower?" Tru Hallihan asked.

Josh glanced up from his cards and covertly surveyed the players gathered around the poker table in the back room at Flynn's. They were all noticeably perplexed, except for Eddie Cassidy, aspiring screenwriter and Flynn's regular bartender. Eddie, the only married member of the group, had joined the game after he took the liquor inventory and now looked ready to provide them all with an explanation.

"Mostly they just sit around and talk," he said. "Then they give the bride a bunch of presents and eat some cake. Then they go home."

Garrett McCabe chuckled and tossed two chips into the pot. "Sounds pretty tame to me. I've heard they sometimes get a male stripper to perform. Just think, Tru, your bride-to-be might be bumping and grinding with some young stud even as we speak. The women's answer to the bachelor party."

Tru scowled. "The wedding shower is at her friend Aurora's house, not at some bar. Besides, I don't think Caroline is the type to—"

"You never know," Garrett said. "Sometimes the quiet ones are the wildest. Take Josh, for example."

Josh smiled at Garrett's good-natured ribbing. "I think Tru is right," Josh said softly. "Caroline doesn't seem the type to enjoy that kind of entertainment." He glanced down at his cards then rearranged them before calling Garrett's raise. "Besides, there are other things that ladies do at a wedding shower."

"How would you know, Banks?" Garrett teased. "Have you ever been to a wedding shower?"

Josh shifted uneasily in his chair. Of all the conversations to choose to participate in, why had he volunteered for this one? Usually, he was a silent participant at the Tuesday night poker games. But after Tru had helped him locate Taryn Wilde, he felt as if he owed a small debt to him. The least he could do was help calm Tru's prewedding jitters and defend his bride's good taste. "As a matter of fact, I've been to three bridal showers. And there wasn't a male stripper in sight."

"So, what *did* they do?" Bob Robinson prodded. Bob, the resident barfly at Flynn's, also served as the resident expert on any number of subjects. But the proper agenda for a wedding shower was beyond even his considerable knowledge of inane trivia.

Josh shrugged. "They do lots of different things, as I recall. I was never formally invited to any of these showers. They were for my older sisters. My mother just brought me along to carry the gifts out to the car when it was over."

"But you saw what goes on, didn't you?" Tru asked.

Josh nodded. He'd seen plenty of what went on. Problem was, he hadn't a clue as to what it all meant. Lots of giggling and gossip, and food that wouldn't satisfy a baby bird's appetite. And of course the requisite teasing from all his female relatives about his looks. *Josh would be so cute if he'd just . . .* the introductory phrase would be followed by any number of suggestions on his hair or his clothes or his introverted personality.

"So, tell us," Garrett urged.

Josh hesitated for a long moment and considered the impact of his explanation. Garrett was always looking for new material and sometimes in the strangest places. He wrote a wildly irreverent column for the *L.A. Post* called "Boys' Night Out", where he extolled the virtues of manhood and regularly lambasted members of the opposite sex, much to the delight of his male readers.

The consummate bachelor, Garrett was everything that Josh was not—smooth with the ladies, a trendy dresser, the type of man every woman found herself drawn to. Josh had often watched him ply his talents at Flynn's, carefully noting Garrett's ease at making small talk with beautiful women. Tru possessed the same ability to manufacture conversation out of thin air. Josh merely hoped that if he hung around with the pair long enough, some of their talent might rub off on him.

"Come on, Josh," Garrett said. "If I use this, I promise not to quote my source."

The Tuesday night poker game at Flynn's had made Garrett's column on a number of occasions, but Josh wasn't sure he wanted to be listed as a major contributor on this particular subject.

"I remember a few things," Josh said reluctantly, "but the last shower I went to was fourteen years ago, when I was seventeen."

"Tell us what you remember," Tru said. "The guests don't try to convince the bride to back out, like they do to the groom at a bachelor party, do they?"

"No. At one of the showers I attended, the guests dressed the bride up in toilet paper," Josh said.

Tru's eyebrows shot up. "Why would they do that?"

"As I understand, they were trying to make a wedding dress out of the stuff. I guess it was supposed to be funny."

"An unusual ritual," Garrett commented.

"And they play a lot of games. I played along once and I won. They gave me an egg timer as a prize and I thought, now here's something I can really use." He looked up to find the group staring at him. "For chess. You know, to time each play. But then the hostess of the shower told me I had to give it to my sister."

"So, they give away prizes, then make you give them to the bride?" Bob asked.

Josh nodded.

Bob's brow knitted in confusion. "What's the point of playing then?" The rest of the group seemed to share Bob's opinion, and Josh had to admit that he did, too. The thought of giving all their poker winnings back at the end of the game made no sense at all.

"And I remember they always had green punch to drink," he added. "And they put it in tiny glass cups that held about two swallows. And when they unwrapped the presents, they took the bows and pasted them on a paper plate, though I'm not quite sure why. And they counted how many ribbons the bride broke as she opened the gifts."

"This sounds too bizarre," Garrett said. "My readers would never believe it. Are you sure you're remembering this right?"

"The number of bows broken is supposed to foretell the number of children the couple will have," Josh explained.

"What?" Tru asked. "You can't be serious!"

"It must work," Josh continued. "My sister Ellen broke three ribbons at her shower and she has three kids. My sister Cindy broke five and she's got five kids."

"But Kim broke three at her wedding shower," Eddie said hopefully, "and we just have one daughter."

"Don't forget, you're still young, Cassidy," Garrett said. "Tru, you'd better hope Caroline isn't too anxious to tear into those presents or you'll be changing diapers for the next ten years."

"Can we change the subject?" Tru asked, his face a bit pale. He took a long swallow of his beer and forced a smile. "Josh, how did it go with Taryn Wilde the other day?"

"Taryn Wilde?" Bob said.

"*You* know Taryn Wilde?" Eddie asked. "*The* Taryn Wilde?"

"Taryn the Terrible?" Garrett chimed in.

"I'm acquainted with her," Josh said. He distractedly counted his chips, stacking and restacking them, while the others waited for more. "Olivia Wilde is a client and Taryn is her granddaughter," Josh explained. "I can't say anything more."

"Don't give us that," Garrett cried. "Last time I checked, tax accountants don't have a code of confidentiality."

Josh looked to Tru and all his friend did was shrug. "Taryn's behavior and Olivia's career are a matter of public knowledge," Tru said. "I don't think you'd be breaking any professional rules."

Josh looked directly at Garrett. "Off the record?" McCabe nodded. "Olivia is worried that any bad press about Taryn might affect her chances for an Oscar nomination," Josh explained. "She asked that I meet with Taryn and convince her to leave town until this whole Academy Award thing is over."

"And did she agree?" Tru asked.

Josh fixed his gaze on his cards. "No."

"What happened?" Tru asked.

"She kicked me out of her apartment. I'm not sure, but I think my approach might have been wrong."

Garrett grinned. "Why don't you let us be the judge of that, Josh," he said. "Tell us all the details."

Josh related the entire conversation as he remembered it, leaving out any reference to Mike, the nude model. "I'll give her some time to consider the situation and I'll visit her again in a few days. I'm certain I can change her mind. With Olivia's permission, I've put together a rather attractive compensation package, tax-free of course, in return for her compliance."

"She won't go," Garrett said.

"Not a chance in hell," Tru added.

Josh turned to Eddie and Bob and they both nodded their agreement.

"You and Olivia have her backed into a corner," Tru said. "Taryn Wilde is not the type of woman who allows anyone to tell her what to do, no matter how attractive the compensation package."

"You see, Josh, a woman like Taryn has spent her life bucking the establishment," Garrett added, "and like it or not, you're the establishment. You probably would have had better luck if you'd insisted she stay in town until the Awards ceremony. She would have left on the next plane just to spite you."

"You're suggesting I use reverse psychology on her?" Josh asked.

"It might work," Tru said.

Garrett nodded in agreement. "Tell her that you and Olivia now believe that any publicity is good publicity and that she's welcome to splash the Wilde name in whatever media she likes."

Josh frowned. "And what if she did just that? Olivia would be the one to suffer. I can't take that chance."

"Then you have only one choice left," Garrett said.

"And what's that?" Josh asked.

"Tie her up," Garrett said.

"Lock her in your apartment," Eddie suggested.

"And don't forget to gag her," Bob said. "You don't want her screaming her head off and waking the neighbors."

Josh looked at Tru for his advice. Tru grinned and clapped Josh on the shoulder. "Short of a massive dose of anesthesia, I'm afraid that's the only way you're going to keep Taryn the Terrible quiet," he said.

Josh winced and shoved his glasses up the bridge of his nose. No, he wouldn't have to resort to anesthesia or bondage. He'd calmly negotiate his terms with Taryn. He'd convince her that it would be best if she left L.A. She would come to understand how much Olivia needed the Oscar recognition. And she would leave without protest.

He drew a deep breath and held it in as he stared at his cards. Tru's words came back to him. *Not a chance in hell.* He exhaled slowly, holding back a long groan. Like it or not, his friends were probably right about Taryn the Terrible. He folded and tossed his cards into the center of the table.

He was definitely in over his head.

JOSH STARED at the digital clock on his office desk as he'd done at least a hundred times that morning. Though he'd made the decision to take a drive over to Taryn's loft and try another round of negotiations, he had neatly managed to find other projects to occupy his time until the morning was nearly gone. The ballots had been mailed two days before and Olivia was due at his office at three for a report. He knew she expected an unqualified success.

He was only avoiding the inevitable. If he didn't make one more attempt, he was certain Taryn would show up again in the tabloids before too long. He didn't trust a promise made over the condition that he simply leave her apartment. Especially after she'd turned down money. He might be a little dense when it came to Taryn Wilde, but he wasn't stupid.

"I'll go this afternoon," he murmured to himself. "Right after lunch." Josh turned back to the files spread across his desk. Losing himself in his work, he'd nearly put Taryn Wilde out of his mind when his intercom buzzer sounded. He picked up the phone and punched the button. "Yes, Delores."

"Mr. Banks, Miss Wilde is here," his secretary informed him.

Before he had a chance to hang up the phone or even wonder why Olivia was four hours early, the door to his office flew open. Taryn stood in the doorway, dressed in a long black skirt, boots that looked as if they came out of an army surplus store, and a bright blue motorcycle jacket, three sizes too big for her. She carried an enormous shoulder bag. Her short-cropped, pale hair was purposely rumpled and her blue-gray eyes sparkled with mischief. She wore no makeup, but still looked incredibly beautiful, fresh and clean and much younger than her twenty-eight years.

"Is the warden in?" she asked, bracing her hands on either side of the doorjamb.

Josh's secretary peeked over Taryn's shoulder and shot him an embarrassed smile. "I'm sorry, Mr. Banks. Miss Wilde said that you'd be expecting her."

"It's all right, Delores." He waited for his secretary to retreat before he turned his attention to Taryn and calmly waited for her to explain herself.

"So tell the truth," she teased. "Were you expecting me?" She waved her hand and stepped into his office. "Don't bother answering. I can tell by that dopey look on your face." She sat down in one of his guest chairs. He noticed that she was wearing what looked like a black bra underneath the leather jacket. Leave it to Taryn to prance around in public in little more than her underwear.

"I was planning to stop by and see you this afternoon," Josh stated. "I thought we might resume our discussion."

"Resume our discussion," she mocked in his serious tone. "Well, I saved you a trip, didn't I?"

He nodded, at a loss for words. She had a strange knack for rendering him speechless. Trying to talk to Taryn Wilde was like trying to communicate with someone from another planet. He'd never met a woman quite like her before, so capricious and unpredictable, and so wholly unsettling.

In the past, he'd had serious relationships with only four women—a fellow tax accountant, a tax lawyer, a financial planner, and a stockbroker, all women he'd met professionally. And though these women were very intelligent and proved to be relatively satisfying in the bedroom, outside the bedroom the relationships never seemed to progress beyond talk of business.

Taryn glanced around the office, then tugged off her jacket and tossed it on the floor. Though the black bra seemed very provocative and revealing at first glance, he noticed that it really wasn't a bra, merely a garment designed to look like one. His gaze followed a line of metal studs that ran along each shoulder strap and met . . . in front.

"Nice place," she commented. "The light's good. The decor's a little too spartan for my tastes, but it seems to suit you."

He searched for an appropriate reply, unable to figure out whether she'd just insulted him or complimented him. "Why do you say that?" he finally asked. All right, it wasn't brilliant conversation, but it would at least keep her talking. He made a mental note to fall back on questions whenever the conversation came to a halt. And to stop looking at her chest.

She pushed out of her chair and walked over to the wall filled with his diplomas and certificates. "Just look at this pitiful composition, Warden. All these nice little frames, exactly the same size, lined up in perfectly straight little rows, just like proper soldiers. This is enough to get you life in prison from the design police." She pulled a frame down from the center of the arrangement, then stepped back and eyed the wall critically. "Much better, don't you think?"

"No. It looks—incomplete now."

She pulled another frame down. "How about now?"

"I don't think that's any better."

She sighed dramatically. "You have no imagination." With that, she methodically began to rearrange the wall, tipping some frames upside down, turning others at a right angle, and twisting some until they were hopelessly crooked. When she stopped, the entire wall looked like the aftereffects of a major earthquake.

He stood up and crossed the room to stare at the mess. "I have a very good imagination," he replied stoically. "I imagine this will take me at least an hour to straighten up."

She stepped back slightly to stand directly in front of him. Resting her hands on her hips, she glanced over her shoulder. "Open your mind to new ideas, Warden. Let that brain of yours out of its tiny little cage. Let it wander around for a while. What do you see?"

He tried to do as she said, but he still didn't see anything but a big mess. Maybe his mind wasn't meant to ponder subjects so mystifying. Although at that moment, his thoughts had willingly wandered from the wall to the woman standing before to him—the biggest mystery of all. She was small, at least eight or nine inches shorter than his six-foot-two height, the top of her head low enough to tuck neatly beneath his chin.

Josh drew a deep, steadying breath and tried to turn his attention back to the wall. She smelled wonderful, like fresh air, spring flowers, and he knew if he stepped just a little closer he could bury his nose in her tousled hair and inhale her scent more deeply, feel the soft strands of pale gold against his cheek and chin.

"Well, what do you see?" she repeated.

Josh snapped out of his daydream and brought his attention back to the chaos on his office wall. "What am I supposed to see?" He had no idea what she was getting at. Was she contending that the mess she made was art? Was it supposed to mean something more than just a bunch of crooked picture frames? Or was she just trying to make him look foolish?

She turned around and looked up at him. Her hand came to rest on his upper arm, and she patted it sympathetically. The warmth of her fingers seeped through the sleeve of his suit jacket and his pulse jumped. "Don't force it, Warden. Maybe you'd better sit down. You look like you're about to pass out." With that, she walked back to the chair and flopped down in it, kicking her leg over one arm. "So, let's cut to the chase. You said you'd planned to come and see me. What were you going to offer me this time?"

Following her suggestion, Josh returned to his desk and tried to regroup. "How do you know I was planning to offer you anything?" he asked. Another question. Good thinking. Keep her talking. He was definitely getting better at this small talk thing.

"You're nothing if you're not predictable. Money, plane tickets, precious jewels, what was it to be this time?" She sighed and shook her head. "Never mind, it really doesn't make a difference. I would have turned you down anyway."

"But you haven't heard the offer yet," Josh said.

"Listen to me carefully, Warden. No amount of money is going to get me out of Los Angeles, not now. There's too much at stake for me here. So you and Olivia had best forget your schemes and learn to live with the disappointment."

"Miss Wilde—"

"Taryn," she corrected. "Miss Wilde is my grandmother."

Josh swallowed hard. "Taryn," he murmured. "As you suggest, let's cut to the chase. If you're not going to leave town, then what is it going to take to ensure your good behavior while you're here?"

"Again with the money. You certainly are a financially retentive man, aren't you?"

Josh stared at her, not certain what she meant.

"You want me to name an amount?" she asked.

"Within reason," Josh replied. "I'd venture to guess that your bank account could use a small infusion of capital right about now."

Taryn's expression froze, her pale blue eyes suddenly turning icy. "What do you know about my bank account?" she shot back.

"I know that you've lived a very...comfortable life in Europe. But that kind of life comes at a price. You can't have much left or you wouldn't have returned to the States."

"My personal financial situation is none of your business, Mr. Banks. Nor is the reason why I returned to the States."

Josh fought back a satisfied grin. At least she'd stopped calling him "Warden." He was making progress. And by the stubborn set of her jaw, he could tell that he'd also come close to hitting the mark. Part of the reason for her return *had* been financial.

"It could be my business, if you'd like," Josh offered. "I help your grandmother manage her money, I could help you, too."

Taryn laughed, a deep, throaty sound that washed over him like warm, bubbling surf. Her eyes were bright and her mouth turned up, like a perfect Cupid's bow. She cupped her chin in her hand and stared at him with mockingly innocent eyes. "I take it back, Warden, you *do* have an imagination . . . deluded as it might be."

"Financial security could make your life much easier," he said.

She sat back in her chair, her expression suddenly distant and unreadable. "Money can't buy happiness," she said.

The trite homily was fraught with meaning and he knew at that moment that any amount he offered would be refused.

"That's the problem with you and Olivia," Taryn continued. "You believe everything in this world can be reduced to the almighty dollar. There are some of us that don't think that way."

"Maybe that's because you've never had to," Josh countered, his mind returning to Olivia's selfless sacrifice for her granddaughter.

She glanced around the office, a patronizing arch to her brow. "And you have?"

"I wasn't born with this," he said.

"Well, maybe if you had been you'd understand how I feel," she replied softly. "Wealth can be as much curse as it can be a blessing." An unusually insecure look settled in her pale eyes. They stared at each other for a long time, the silence between them growing. Josh shifted uneasily in his chair and let out a tightly held breath. This was not going well.

"All right," he conceded. "You tell me. What will it take?" What *would* make a woman like Taryn Wilde happy? He searched his mind, but beyond money, he could think of nothing. What could she possibly value if not financial security?

A sly smile quirked her lips, her mood suddenly shifting like sunlight glinting on the Pacific. "There is one thing that would make it easier for me to stay home and behave," she said.

"Name it," Josh replied.

"I want you to pose for me," Taryn said.

Josh frowned. He was nearly certain he had misunderstood her words. "You want what?" he asked.

"I want you to pose for me," Taryn repeated. "Nude, of course."

He gasped. "You must be joking."

Taryn shook her head. "I'm not. You asked me what I wanted and I told you. That's the deal, Warden. You get naked, I paint your picture. Oh, and you might as well know, this could take some time."

"You already have a model," Josh countered. "What about Mike?"

"Mike isn't exactly what I was looking for. He's too . . . easy."

Easy? What the hell was that supposed to mean? He'd heard about girls in high school who were "easy." Certainly, she didn't mean the same thing. Maybe it was some kind of art term. "And *I'm* what you're looking for?" Josh asked.

"Exactly," Taryn replied with a smug smile. "You have these wonderful layers of complexity and I have a real desire to strip you bare. Metaphorically speaking, that is."

Josh forced a smile. "This is all very amusing, Taryn, and I'm sure that you're deriving a great deal of enjoyment from your little game, but—"

"It's not a game," Taryn said. She bent over the arm of the chair and grabbed her jacket, then stood up. "That's the deal. You scratch my back, I'll scratch yours." The last was said with more than a hint of innuendo. She hoisted her bag onto her shoulder and strolled to the door, then turned around to give him one more devastating smile.

"You know where I live," she said. "I'll be expecting you...soon." With that she pulled open his office door and walked out.

Josh stared at the door, once again, rendered totally speechless. He pulled off his glasses and rubbed his eyes with the heels of his hands. She couldn't possibly be serious. The thought of taking off his clothes in front of Taryn Wilde brought only one image to mind—and it certainly didn't include *her* remaining fully clothed. No, if he got naked in Taryn's loft, there would be much, *much* more than painting to look forward to.

Josh smiled and shook his head. Leave it to Taryn the Terrible to tease him in such a clever way. No, she wasn't serious. She couldn't be. Josh's humor faded slightly.

Or could she?

THREE DAYS AFTER her visit to Josh's office, Taryn was still waiting for Josh Banks to show up at the loft. The creative juices had already begun to churn inside her and she was anxious to get to work. She had applied gesso to three large canvases and had spent a minor fortune on a set of new sable brushes in preparation. Since early that morning, she had been pacing the loft, restless and impatient and thoroughly frustrated. She had called his office, but when his answering service picked up, she realized that it was Saturday and he probably wasn't working. She had finally decided to call his home number when her security buzzer sounded.

With a cry of glee, Taryn ran over to the control panel and pushed the button. She stood by the door, anxiously awaiting his knock. When it finally came, she peeked out the peephole. But the figure standing outside in the hallway was not that of Josh Banks. She pulled the door open and her heart fell.

"*Chérie! C'est moi!* All your troubles are *finis.* Your Berti is here to take you away from this—" Bertrand-Remy Ducharme stepped inside the door and looked around the loft. "This—" He frowned. "Well, I'm not sure what the word for this place is. But I'm here to take you away from it, whatever it is." In the blink of an eye, he had gathered her in his arms and picked her up off the floor.

"Berti," she gasped, his hug nearly cutting off her oxygen. "What are you doing here?" Bertrand dropped her to her feet and held her at arm's length.

"Ah, I have missed you, *chérie,*" he gushed. "Ever since you have left I am a basket cake."

Dismayed as she was, Taryn couldn't help but laugh. Berti's fractured attempts at American slang had always been his most endearing feature. They'd known each other for two years and since the day Margaux had introduced them in Monaco, the Frenchman had professed to be madly in love with her—even though she gave him absolutely no reciprocation.

"See there," Berti boasted. "You are happy to see me, *non?*"

A playboy of the first order, Bertrand-Remy Ducharme had been a member-in-good-standing of her glamorous circle of jet-setting friends. His career in Grand Prix racing, largely financed by his wealthy, indulgent parents, gave him a very dashing reputation with the ladies. But though he was infinitely charming and exceedingly handsome, Berti was also vain, self-absorbed, spoiled, and just a tad obtuse.

Even so, he had been an amusing and devoted companion, always there to boost her ego when it needed a lift. She had strung him along while he chased her all over Europe, until their final breakup, the night before she left for the States.

She should have expected that he would follow her here. Like a child, Berti considered her a possession he could not attain, thereby making her all the more attractive. The more she resisted him, the more persistent and petulant he became. She had made her feelings quite clear when they parted, but obviously Berti couldn't take a hint.

"If you came all the way from France to rescue me, then you *are* a basket cake. I'm not returning to Europe."

"Do not tell me this, *chérie*. I have been despondent since you deserted me. I cannot think of anything but you. I came here to tell you that you were very right. I admit, I do have a head like a pig."

Taryn shook her head. "I didn't say that. I told you that you were pigheaded. Stubborn and single-minded."

"Yes, that too. Now, are you going to invite me to come in, Tara? Or must I stand here and gravel?"

"Grovel," Taryn corrected. "And no, you don't have to grovel. Come in."

Berti rushed back out the door and returned with a garment bag and a suitcase. "I love this city," he said. "On my way from the airport, I think I see the Terminator." He tossed his bags on the floor and threw himself on the couch. "I am too tired to be dead. Come here and give your Berti a kiss."

Taryn sat down on the coffee table. "Bertrand, where do you plan to stay while you're here?"

"Why, with you, Tara, where else?"

Taryn ran her fingers through her hair and sighed. "I have a lot of work to do before my opening. I don't have time to entertain you. You'll really have to stay at a hotel."

He shot her a disarming smile. "I will as be quiet as a moose," Berti said. "You will not know I am here."

Taryn groaned inwardly. He was right—he had a head like a pig, and there would be no changing his mind. His parents had raised him well—what Berti wanted, Berti got. "Three days," she said. "That's it. You'll sleep in the guest room. But then you'll have to find another place to stay." Berti was part of her old life and the sooner she got rid of him, the easier it would be to concentrate on her painting. Still, she dreaded telling him, once again, that it was over between them. Berti rarely took no for an answer.

"We will see," he replied. "Now, I am so hungry I could eat my horse. What do you have here to feed me?"

"I don't have much in the refrigerator," Taryn said tartly. "I wasn't expecting a houseguest."

"No matter," he said, bouncing up off the couch. "We will go find something. I would like some American food. A hot dog, or maybe a taco. And for dessert, I would like an apple pie."

Taryn stood and smiled, then walked toward the dining area. "You did not come to the States to eat your way through the junk food aisles. You can do that at home." She grabbed her scarf and a floppy straw hat from the table. "We'll go to the grocery store and get something healthy. Then we have to come right home. I'm expecting . . . company."

She wasn't ready to give up on Josh Banks, not yet. Though, if he didn't show today, she wasn't sure what she'd be able to do about it. She couldn't force him to take his clothes off.

A half hour later, they pulled into the parking lot of Food Faire, a large gourmet grocery store in Beverly Hills. Berti had wanted to drive, but Taryn knew his penchant for speed and was adamant that the VW convertible Margaux had lent her was not insured for Grand Prix drivers.

They had nearly filled a shopping cart with his choices and she was putting together a fresh salad from the salad bar when she noticed the photographer standing near the gourmet mushrooms. She ducked her head and pulled the brim of her hat lower, a movement borne of instinct, then hurried to finish building her salad. Berti stepped to her side and a camera flash went off. He looked up and smiled.

"There is a man who wants to take our photograph, *chérie*. Smile."

"Just ignore him," she whispered.

Suddenly the photographer was standing on the other side of the salad bar. The camera flashed again. "Hey, Taryn, who's your boyfriend?" the photographer shouted. He scrambled closer and the camera began to flash incessantly.

"Peasant!" Berti muttered through a tight smile. "He does not know who I am?"

"Leave us alone!" Taryn cried.

She wasn't sure exactly what happened next. Somehow, the photographer ended up sprawled on the floor with a huge bowl of romaine lettuce spilled over his chest. Taryn grabbed his camera and extracted the film, exposing the length of it before smearing it with Italian dressing. The flash found a home in the Roquefort dressing before she twisted off the lens and dropped it into a crock of French onion soup. Meanwhile, Berti regaled the man, and a large group of interested shoppers, with vivid French epithets. The police arrived shortly after the photographer struggled to his feet—just in time to watch Taryn whack the photographer squarely in the nose with her bag, sending him down for the count.

Witnesses were interviewed while she and Berti sat in the back of the police car. The Saturday crowd at the grocery store found the whole scene endlessly fascinating and milled around in the parking lot, waiting for more. She slumped down in the seat and kept her eyes peeled for more photographers.

"This is it," Berti moaned. "We will go to the pig house and have to work on the shame gang."

"We will not be sent up the river to the *big* house, Bertrand. And it's *chain* gang, not shame gang. You've seen way too many Dirty Harry movies for your own good."

"You think we will meet Dirty Harry?" he asked, genuine excitement in his voice. "I love his movies. He has such large . . . how do you say? Guns?"

Taryn leaned back and closed her eyes. Why was this happening to her? She'd already decided to keep a low profile in Los Angeles, and not because of her grandmother or Josh Banks, but because of the gallery opening. She didn't want the opening to turn into the same kind of circus that seemed to trail her around Europe. She wanted serious art collectors, not curiosity seekers, to view her work. She wanted respectful appreciation, not amused interest.

The police officer returned to the car and slipped into the driver's seat. Taryn sat up and waited for his verdict. "The store is willing to settle for reparations. The photographer says he'll drop the charges under one condition," the officer explained.

"What's that?" Taryn asked.

"You pay for the damage to his camera and agree to give him an interview. He works for the *Inquisitor*. It's up to you, Miss Wilde. You can walk away from this now, or I can take you down to the station and book you."

"What about Bertrand?"

"Mr. Ducharme is free to go now. The guy didn't want to press charges against him."

"And if I decide to refuse his offer and go down to the station? What will happen then?"

"We'll book you for battery and malicious mischief. You can post bail and be out in about an hour."

"How much?"

"Twenty-five hundred."

Taryn winced and considered the trade-off. Another tabloid article or twenty-five hundred dollars. "I guess we're going down to the station, officer. I'm not about to give that tabloid worm word one."

The officer smiled and started the squad car. "Do you want Mr. Ducharme to bring your car?"

"No," Taryn answered. "He can't drive."

"What do you mean, I cannot drive!" Berti huffed. "I am Bertrand-Remy Ducharme. I won the Grand Prix de—"

"Berti, please," she interrupted. "Just relax and enjoy the ride while I figure out what to do."

If she was lucky—and she sincerely hoped that for once in her life she would be—the debacle at Food Faire wouldn't make it into the tabloids without a good photo. Taryn groaned inwardly. How could she have gotten herself into this mess? It was as if all her good intentions had suddenly disappeared when the photographer stuck his camera in her face. An overwhelming instinct to defend herself had rushed through her. Maybe it wouldn't be so easy to leave her past behind, especially when her old behaviors kept popping up unexpectedly.

She'd just have to find a way to extract herself from this mess without any more publicity. Calling Margaux for help was out; she would not let the gallery owner doubt her professionalism for a minute. Berti had seven dollars in cash with him and an American Express card, which the police probably didn't take, so he wouldn't be of much help either. Her checking account was nearly dry, her credit cards too close to being maxed out.

An hour later, as she sat in the holding cell, waiting for her one phone call, an option occurred to her. This whole ridiculous incident could actually work to her advantage. That was it! The idea was brilliant in its simplicity. She'd call Josh Banks and force him to post her bail. He'd be angry, frustrated and ready to do anything to make her behave.

And after that, he'd just have to agree to pose for her.

3

TARYN PACED the confines of the holding cell, her temper growing with each step. She'd made her one phone call three hours ago, to Josh's home number, and got his damn answering service again. She had left a highly detailed message, but since then, she'd heard nothing.

At first, she'd hoped her arrest might just be the push he needed to agree to her deal. He'd pay her fine, she'd appear properly contrite, and she'd promise to behave—as long as he posed for her. But she'd been stuck in the holding cell for much longer than she'd ever intended, and she was getting downright furious.

She could picture him lounging around at home right this minute, watching a ball game or reading a magazine, and getting a good laugh from her predicament. Maybe he had even called Olivia to tell her the good news. They were probably overjoyed to leave her right where she was. At least in jail, she couldn't get into any more trouble.

Though she was having a perfectly miserable Saturday afternoon, Berti was enjoying himself thoroughly. He'd talked the arresting officer into giving him a tour of the station, had participated in a lineup, whined until they took his mug shot and fingerprints as a souvenir, and had generally made a pest of himself.

She'd given him Josh's phone number and all the change in the bottom of her purse and demanded that he call Josh's service at least every ten minutes. The last she'd seen of him, he was on his way to view the firing range in the basement of the station. And she strongly suspected the candy bar he was munching on had been purchased with her phone money.

Taryn swore softly. The next time Berti decided to give her an update on his entertaining day, she'd give *him* a piece of her mind. She'd also give him cab fare and send him to see Margaux. Even she was ready to admit that it was time to abandon her plan and find another way to post bail. Frustrated and more than a little bit embarrassed, Taryn sat down on the cot and buried her face in her hands. How had she managed to get herself into another mess?

Footsteps echoed against the concrete walls of the cell block. The sound stopped in front of Taryn's cell and she slowly looked up—from highly polished black wingtips to finely pressed trousers, from an exquisitely tailored jacket to a red silk tie, and right up to Josh Banks's inscrutable expression.

Taryn stifled a cry of relief. He had come! He was late, but he'd still come. And her plan might work yet. Gathering her wits, she leaned back on the cot and stretched indolently, hiding a yawn behind her hand. "Why hello, Warden," she said, trying to sound nonchalant. "Come to check up on your favorite prisoner?"

Josh studied her for a long moment, his gaze riveted on hers, his expression as intractable as a marble statue. A shiver skittered up her spine and she forced herself to look away. She'd never noticed what gorgeous eyes he had behind those conservative glasses. Dark and warm and liquid, framed with disgustingly long lashes for a man. Eyes that provided the only window to his soul.

"The nickname suddenly seems appropriate," he muttered, taking in her surroundings.

Taryn pushed off the cot and sauntered toward the cell door. "I know how happy you must be to see me incarcerated but you didn't have to dress for the occasion. Tell me, do you sleep in those suits of yours?"

Josh's jaw tightened. "I didn't expect to be called down to the police station," he said. "I was attending a wedding."

She wrapped her fingers around the bars and leaned toward him. "Not yours, I hope?" she teased.

He drew a deep breath, drawing his body up to its full height. He was trying to look authoritative, Taryn mused. "Would you care to explain what you're doing in here, Taryn?" he asked, irritation seeping into his cool tone.

Taryn. He couldn't be that mad at her or he would have called her Miss Wilde. "Didn't the police give you the whole story?" she asked.

"They did," he replied, "but I'd like to hear your version."

She waved her hand distractedly. "It was all a silly misunderstanding," she said. "A disagreement over a few photographs. I was grocery shopping, minding my own business, when this loathsome tabloid photographer started to get into my business. I was simply protecting my right to privacy."

Josh pushed his suit jacket back and braced his hands on his hips, his brow furrowed. "Taryn, this is exactly the kind of trouble I wanted you to avoid. Do you have any idea how this will look once it hits the papers?"

At that precise moment, he sounded exactly like the old headmistress at her Swiss boarding school, a pinch-faced woman she'd come to detest in her years there. "Are you concerned about me," Taryn asked, "or do you only care about how this will affect Olivia?"

"Any negative publicity associated with the Wilde name could only hurt Olivia. You know that."

"So you *are* only concerned about Olivia," Taryn said.

Josh hesitated before he answered her, his silence echoing through the jail cell. "No," he finally replied. "I'm concerned about you, too. I don't want to see you hurt and if you continue on this self-destructive path, you will be."

Though Taryn knew her first reaction should have been outrage at his patronizing attitude, she found herself strangely pleased by his admission. She'd never really had anyone in her life who was truly concerned about her welfare. To her parents, she was just an inconvenience, to her grandmother, a burden. Most of her "friends" merely cared about her money or her reputation, not about her. She couldn't count how many people had stood in the circle of celebrity that surrounded her, yet not one of them could she call in a time of crisis. Until Josh Banks.

"So, you *do* care about me?" Taryn asked, suddenly needing confirmation.

"Of course," he snapped. "It's just that no one is going to know this incident was just a silly misunderstanding. They'll only remember it was bad news. The Academy voters are very impressionable and I—"

Taryn pushed away from the cell door. "Are you through with your lecture now?" she asked, her voice filled with icy impatience. All right, so she'd misread his concern. He didn't really care about her. And wasn't any different from all the others in her life. "Because if you are, maybe it's time to start examining your own hand in all this."

"My hand?" He regarded her suspiciously, his dark eyes narrowed.

"I offered to keep a low profile, in fact, I promised to stay holed up in my apartment if you agreed to pose for me."

"You were serious?" Josh gasped.

"Of course I was serious! This whole mess could have been avoided if you would have bothered to stop by the loft for a sitting. Right now, I'd be hard at work on my paintings rather than holding court in some high-class hoosegow."

"I told you before, I am not going to take my clothes off and let you paint me," Josh said. "You can forget that idea right now."

She heaved a dramatic sigh, then turned to survey the cell. "Well, I guess I might as well familiarize myself with these surroundings, because I'm sure I'll be back here for another visit soon."

"I could leave you in here," Josh threatened, his customary cool now showing signs of cracking. "A little jail time would probably do you a world of good."

"It's never worked in the past," Taryn said sweetly. "Why would it suddenly work now?"

Josh rubbed his forehead, a tiny muscle in his jaw twitching with each stroke of his fingers. She suspected he really wanted to yell and swear and pitch a screaming fit, but he was too damn polite to do it in front of a woman. "If I agree to bail you out, I at least want some assurance that you'll behave yourself."

"I'm very willing to discuss the terms of our deal in greater detail," Taryn said. "But not from inside a jail cell."

"All right," Josh replied, his voice terse. "I'll be back for you after I pay your bail. How much is it?"

"Twenty-five hundred."

"Twenty-five hundred," he repeated, his voice edged with exasperation. He shook his head. "Do you think you can at least stay out of trouble until I get back?"

"What kind of trouble could I possibly get in here?" Taryn asked, wide-eyed with mock innocence.

"I do seem to recall an incident where you assaulted a policeman," Josh said. "That story made the front pages of an Italian newspaper."

Taryn's temper flared. "That was not my fault!" she cried. "I never meant to hit him. You see, I borrowed this dress from a designer friend and then Roberto spilled red wine all over it and then—" She stopped abruptly. She didn't owe him an explanation! "That incident was blown totally out of proportion," she finished calmly.

"As I'm sure this one will be, as well. Much to the disappointment of your grandmother."

"Listen, Warden, I'm getting a little tired of your sermons. Either bail me out or leave me here, but quit pontificating."

"Fine," Josh bit out as he walked toward the door.

He'd been gone nearly thirty minutes before Taryn realized that maybe he *did* intend to leave her in jail. A surge of relief rushed through her a few moments later when he reappeared at the cell door with an imposing policewoman—Officer J. Knowles by her name tag. The woman was nearly six feet tall and well muscled, but her rather formidable physique was balanced by a sweet face and a warm smile. She unlocked the cell door and motioned Taryn out.

"You're free to go," she said. "Mr. Banks has paid your fine. Mr. Ducharme is waiting for you in the lobby." She leaned closer to Taryn. "The chief was almost ready to waive the fine, just to get rid of Bertrand," she confided. "No one's gotten much work done this afternoon."

Taryn smiled. "I'm sorry," she whispered back. "He can be a real pest."

Officer Knowles chuckled. "A very charming pest." Taryn thought she detected a slight blush in the woman's cheeks. Berti had been up to his usual tricks, it seemed.

As the policewoman promised, Berti was waiting for her in the lobby. The instant he spotted her, he rushed up and gathered her in his arms. She turned to look behind her and found Josh watching with mild interest.

"*Chérie*, what an ordeal! Are you all right?"

"I'm fine, Berti," she replied, pulling out of his grasp.

"I am glad to hear it. Look at this!" he said with the excitement of a child. He held out a small stack of photos, the top one of himself in profile against a lined wall. "These are shootings of my mug."

"Very nice," Taryn commented.

"I am so handsome. But I look dangerous, no?"

"No," she said wryly. "Come on, let's get out of here. Josh is going to take us home. I want to take a long, hot bath. Then we'll go get the car and get some dinner."

"Josh?" Berti asked. "Who is this Josh person?"

Josh stepped closer and she turned to him. "Josh Banks, this is my friend, Bertrand-Remy Ducharme. Bertrand, this is Josh Banks."

Berti studied Josh shrewdly, his arm slipping possessively around Taryn's waist. When he had determined that the man was no competition, he held out his hand. "Banks, it is a pleasure to meet you. *Un ami* of Tara's is *un ami* of mine."

Josh shook Berti's hand. "A pleasure to meet you, too, Bert."

Taryn hid her amusement as Berti bristled at the seemingly innocuous misunderstanding of his name. Had Josh heard the name wrong, or had he also sized up the competition and found his weaknesses? Josh didn't seem to be the type to play games, but she certainly wouldn't put it past him.

"It is Bertrand," the Frenchman said through clenched teeth. "B-E-R-T-R-A-N-D. Not Bert. And only Berti to my closest friends. I am French, of course. My name is Bertrand-Remy Ducharme."

Josh shrugged. "Sorry."

Berti studied Josh for a long moment, as if he were waiting for further comment. "What? You do not recognize me?" he asked.

"Should I?" Josh asked.

Berti cursed vividly in French. "Does no one know Grand Prix in this country? My name is Bertrand-Remy Ducharme. *The* Bertrand-Remy Ducharme."

Josh looked at him blankly. "Yes, I understand that. And you're a friend of Taryn's. From France."

On overload, Berti's ego finally blew a fuse and Taryn saw a petulant expression settle on his face, an expression she'd learned to be very wary of. "Not just a friend," he said, calculatingly watching for Josh's reaction. "I am Taryn's *amant*, her *amoureux*. Her...how you say... lover?"

She looked to Josh, ready to refute Berti's boast, but the words caught in her throat. A unbidden stab of disappointment shot through her as Josh showed absolutely no reaction at all to Berti's comment. Just what had she expected? Surprise? Aggravation? Jealousy? And why would she even *care* what Josh Banks felt?

"You are not my lover," Taryn said, shooting Berti a censorious glare.

"Well, I will be, *chérie*. It is a *fait accompli, non?*"

"No, it is not." She turned to Josh. "He's not my lover. He's just a friend."

Josh shrugged again in that same noncommittal way that was really starting to bug her. "It's none of my business who you spend your time with, Taryn. I'm merely concerned about *how* you spend your time. Now, go collect your things so I can take you and Bert home. I have to get back to the wedding."

Her fingernails biting into her palms, Taryn forced back a stinging retort and stalked past Josh to where Officer Knowles had laid her belongings on the counter. She picked through the contents of her purse as she silently chastised herself.

How could she have been so stupid as to believe in his false concern? He wasn't her friend and he didn't care about *her* at all. He only cared about curbing her unruly behavior and pleasing her domineering grandmother. He was nothing but a stuffy old autocrat, intent on his prim and proper agenda.

By now, she should have been able to spot a phony a mile a way. She'd spent the past eight years among them. It was just that she'd never expected Josh Banks to fall into that category. He seemed so honest and dependable. So . . . normal.

After she had signed for her purse, she hoisted it on her shoulder and walked to the front door of the station. "Come on, Warden," she said as she tugged on her hat. "I don't want to waste any more of your precious time."

Berti followed her, with Josh trailing behind him. "Yes, come on, Ward," Berti ordered. "We are ready to blow on this joint now."

THE RIDE TO THE LOFT passed in silence for both Josh and Taryn. Bert chattered on from the back seat in a mixture of French and English, carrying on a one-sided conversation that recounted his afternoon at the Beverly Hills police station. Every few blocks, Josh risked a glance over at Taryn. She stared straight ahead, her ashen expression a mixture of tightly leashed tension and emotional exhaustion.

She had good cause to be upset, Josh mused. As soon as they had walked out the front door of the police station, three photographers had appeared, pushing and shoving against each other to get a photo of Taryn, shouting questions and accusations until she had to cover her ears. He'd fought them off, shielding her from their cameras until he could get her inside the car.

But when the photographers swooped down on them like a pack of vultures at a picnic, old Berti had simply turned and smiled, pleased by all the attention. Josh glanced up into the rearview mirror and covertly observed Ducharme. What could she possibly see in the egotistical Frenchman? A man was supposed to protect those he loved. Bert would still be standing there, posing for pictures, if Josh hadn't grabbed him and shoved him into the back seat of the Volvo.

Josh looked back at Taryn and cursed silently. She looked so weak and defenseless, not at all like the Taryn he knew. If this was what she had to put up with in Europe, it was no wonder she'd fled. The photographers stopped just short of assault in their quest to get a good photo. And if Taryn had been alone, there would have been no way to avoid the inevitable, another picture on the front page of another tabloid. Suddenly, her behavior in the supermarket didn't seem quite so rash.

After what they'd experienced in front of the police station, Josh had been surprised when the photographers made no attempt to trail his car. But as they pulled up to Taryn's loft, he realized why. Three more photographers were camped out on the street in front of the converted warehouse.

The moment Taryn saw the trio, a tiny cry of dismay escaped her lips and she sank down into the seat, covering her face. "No," she moaned. "How did they find out where I live?"

"Don't worry," Josh said. He glanced over his shoulder and made a quick U-turn, then watched the retreating scene in his rearview mirror. "I don't think they saw us."

"They're not going to go away," she said dismally. "You might as well turn around and go back. We'll face them now and let them get their damn pictures. Then maybe they'll leave me alone."

"No," Josh said firmly. "We're not going back. I'm not going to let them invade your privacy again. They have no right to do that to you."

"They think they have every right," Taryn shot back.

"Well, they're wrong. We'll come back later tonight," Josh said, "and hopefully they'll be gone."

"And if they're not?" she asked.

"We'll cross that bridge when we come to it."

She stared at him, her brow creased, her pale eyes questioning. "Why are you doing this?"

Why? He was tempted to tell her the truth—that he wanted to save her from the torment that the photographers obviously caused her. Or that he wanted to spend more time with her. Or that he wanted her to learn to trust him. But he chose the easy way out. "I don't want to see your picture in the papers," he said.

"Is that all it is?" Taryn asked.

"What more would it be?"

"I don't know," she said, her voice mirroring her exhaustion. "For a second there, I thought you might be developing a noble streak, Warden."

Josh couldn't help but smile at her backhanded compliment. "Would that surprise you?" he asked.

"You have many strange and fascinating layers, Warden." She paused, the corners of her mouth turning up mischievously. "You know, someone should really try to capture that on canvas."

"And you have a one-track mind," he said with a laugh. Josh turned his attention back to the road. But his thoughts wandered to the woman beside him. She seemed fixated on this need to paint him. At first, he'd thought it was some kind of joke, but Taryn wouldn't let the subject die. She really did want to paint him.

He imagined himself in her loft, undressing behind the Chinese screen. But then the image shifted, taking a different tack. Taryn was there, but her clothes were on the floor at her feet. Then their bodies were twined together on the rumpled bed, her brushes and canvases forgotten, as they lost themselves in each other.

"All right, what if I told you you could wear some clothes?"

Startled out of his contemplation, Josh snapped his gaze back to her. "Some clothes? What are you talking about?"

"Our deal," she said. "Back at the jail you said that you'd consider posing for me. And I'm saying that I might allow you to wear some clothes."

"Some clothes?" he asked. "What clothes in particular?"

"That's up for negotiation," she said.

"And what if I agree? Then you'll promise to keep a low profile until after the awards?"

"The level of my profile will be in direct proportion to the level of your nakedness."

Josh stared out the windshield. "I'll think about it," he acquiesced. He'd think about it all right. The truth was, he hadn't stopped thinking about it since she'd first mentioned the idea. He'd think about it as he stared at his computer screen at work, imagining the sweet smell of her hair and the silkiness of her skin, and trying to recall the exact color of her eyes. He'd think about it lying in bed at night, wondering what it would feel like to have Taryn in his arms, what her body might feel like beneath his.

Taryn pushed up in the seat and stared at him, surprised. "You'll think about it? Really?"

"Yes," Josh replied, swallowing convulsively. "Really."

She sat back in the seat, a satisfied expression on her face. "I'll settle for that. For now. So, where are we going?"

"I'm going to take you to my apartment. We'll order some dinner and you and Bert can stay there while I put in a quick appearance at the wedding reception. When I get back, I'll take you home."

"Who's wedding?" she asked.

"My friend, Tru Hallihan, and Dr. Caroline Leighton."

Another grin quirked the corners of her mouth. He liked to watch her smile. Her eyes grew bright and her perfect lips curled at the corners. It was like watching fireworks on the Fourth of July. Dazzling. Breathtaking. And all too long between the next show.

"You could always take us along," she suggested.

He glanced over at her in amazement, then shook his head. "I just bailed you out of jail and you expect me to take you along to a friend's wedding? I'm not about to compound one error in judgment with another."

"I promise I won't cause any trouble," Taryn said. "Cross my heart." She drew an *X* on her chest. "Come on, Warden, I've been shut up in that damn loft for days. I'd love a party. I *need* a party."

"This isn't a party, it's a wedding reception," Josh countered.

"And this a chance for me to prove that I really *can* behave...if I put my mind to it."

Josh smiled grimly. "I don't need proof. I'm quite certain you could to just about anything you wanted to . . . if you put your mind to it."

"Then you'll take us?"

"Us?"

"We'll have to take Berti," she explained. "But don't worry, he knows how to behave at parties." She grinned. "He usually keeps *me* out of trouble."

"Forgive me if I don't find that of much comfort."

"Please?" Taryn begged. "Weddings are such fun. I just love to drink champagne and dance the night away."

"That's exactly what I'm afraid of," Josh said. "Besides, you're not dressed for a wedding."

Taryn stuck out her lower lip in a pretty pout. "What's wrong with what I'm wearing? This is perfectly fine." He turned to glance at her. She wore a crinkled yellow dress, with wide bell sleeves and modestly cut neckline. A long, colorful scarf was wrapped around and around her neck and tossed over her shoulders. A floppy straw hat with big flowers around the brim rested in her lap. From black leather and combat boots to a sixties garden party, Taryn did have a flair for contradictory fashion statements. He had to admit, she did look pretty nice. Maybe she was right. Or maybe he was just starting to get used to the way she dressed.

"Just because you always wear a suit, doesn't mean the rest of us have to dress so formally," Taryn said. "Do you ever take that stuffy old outfit off?"

"I've been known to sleep in a suit," Josh explained.

A bubble of laughter escaped Taryn's lips. Josh shot her a sideways glance. He hadn't meant the statement to be funny. There were many times when he had worked late at the office and woke up the next morning to find himself stretched out on his office couch, still fully dressed.

Josh listened to her giggle, the sound like music on a summer breeze. First, his conversational skills took a sudden turn for the better and now he'd actually shown signs of a sense of humor. What was next? Posing naked for Taryn Wilde? Or maybe...

Josh shook his head, pushing the notion from his mind. He'd be crazy to take her to the wedding. Where was his common sense when he needed it most? It seemed to disappear the instant he saw Taryn smile, heard her laugh. Josh stifled a moan. Heaven help him for what he was about to do. "All right," he said. "You and Bert can come along. But the first sign of trouble and we'll be out of there faster than—"

"A duck in a dune buggy," Bert piped up from the back seat.

Josh frowned, staring at the man in the rearview mirror.

"Don't bother asking him," Taryn whispered. "I think he meant 'faster than a duck on a June bug.'"

"Thank you for the translation," Josh replied.

"No problem." With a sigh of contentment, Taryn turned to gaze out the passenger side window, her hands neatly folded in her lap, a perfectly virtuous expression on her face. The fatigue that marked her features just minutes before had disappeared and her complexion had regained some of its color.

Josh glanced over at her now and then as he wove back through the streets of Beverly Hills and headed up Laurel Canyon Boulevard, curious as to her mercurial moods. First, she was happy to see him, then she was suddenly angry, and then she was teasing and cajoling him—and now he had no idea what was running through that mind of hers. He wanted very much to believe it wasn't trouble.

He had his doubts whether Taryn could actually control her behavior. She seemed to thrive on spontaneity and high emotion, action and immediate reaction. And whether she craved the attention or not, the tabloid press was determined to record her every audacious move. The problem was, Josh couldn't always be there to stand between Taryn and general mayhem.

If he could only trust her promise, maybe he might consider a trade—her cooperation for his semi-naked body. When he had explained to Olivia that her granddaughter would not accept money to leave town, the older woman's spirits tumbled to an all-time low. Josh had vowed to Olivia that he would do his best to deal with Taryn, no matter what it took. And after all, she had conceded that he wouldn't have to remove *all* his clothes.

"Thank you," she said softly.

Josh turned, wondering if he'd only imagined her speaking. "Did you say something?"

"Thank you," she repeated.

"For what?"

"For turning out to be a nice guy after all."

Baffled, Josh turned away. "You're welcome," he replied, unsure of what she meant and unable to think of any other reply.

The wedding reception was in full swing when they arrived. An uneasy feeling of apprehension assailed Josh as he headed up the front walk to the door, Taryn and Bert at his heels. Just how would he explain Taryn's presence? Or Ducharme's for that matter? Though his invitation had indicated he could bring a guest, he was sure that the bride and groom didn't expect a notorious party girl and French race car driver with an insolent attitude.

As they stepped through the front door, the first sight he saw was the bride and her groom. Caroline Leighton stood on the far side of the sunken living room, dressed in a lovely old-fashioned dress, layered with lace from her shoulders to her ankles. Tru stood at her side, looking very respectable and a bit uncomfortable in a suit and tie. Wedding guests surrounded the couple, laughing and talking in subdued enjoyment. A pianist played a soft ballad as a few guests danced.

To his surprise, no one turned to look as they entered. The room didn't grow silent, then buzz with speculation. Cameras didn't flash and guests didn't gasp. Josh straightened his tie and stepped out of the shadow of the foyer.

"If they have no caviar here," he heard Bert whisper from behind him, "we will go home."

Josh glanced over his shoulder and directed a narrow-eyed glare in the Frenchman's direction.

Taryn looped her arm through Ducharme's and stepped to Josh's side. "Just behave yourself, Berti, and be nice," Taryn ordered. She slanted a smile in Josh's direction. "I promised Josh."

"Josh!"

Startled by the shout, Josh's attention snapped back to the reception and he watched as Tru and Caroline wove their way through the guests toward the new arrivals.

"Where did you wander off to?" Tru asked. "We were starting to get worried."

Josh looked over at Taryn and Bert. "I had to go pick up my...date," he said.

"At the Beverly Hills jail," Taryn added beneath her breath, just loud enough for Josh to hear. Berti merely snorted, then mumbled something in French.

Josh forced a smile. "Tru and Caroline, I'd like you to meet Taryn Wilde." He turned to Taryn. "Taryn, this is my friend, Tru Hallihan, and his bride, Dr. Caroline Leighton Hallihan."

He expected exclamations of surprise or at least recognition from the bride and groom, but there were none. Caroline held out her hand to Taryn, smiling warmly. "It's a pleasure to meet you, Taryn. I'm so glad you could join us. We didn't expect Josh to bring a date." If she knew who Taryn was, she obviously didn't care.

Taryn shook Caroline's hand. "Josh's invitation was a bit last minute," she said demurely. "I'm sorry if I'm not dressed properly or if I've intruded."

"Don't be silly," Tru said. "Josh's friends are always welcome here." For a long moment, they all stood there, looking at each other expectantly. Then Tru turned to Ducharme and held out his hand. "I'm Tru Hallihan."

Josh jumped in at that moment, suddenly aware of his lack of manners. It was so satisfying to just forget Berti. "And this is Taryn's . . ." He paused, not quite sure what Ducharme really meant to Taryn. The hell if he was going to introduce the pesky Frenchman as her lover. "Friend," Josh finished. "Bert. He's visiting from France."

"Bertrand-Remy Ducharme," the Frenchman corrected.

Tru looked at Josh, then back at Berti, clearly astonished by the introduction. "*The* Bertrand Ducharme? The Grand Prix driver?"

A smile split Bert's supercilious expression. "Yes! You know of me?"

"I do," Tru replied. "And I have some friends who would love to meet you." He kissed Caroline on the cheek. "Sweetheart, I'll be right back. I want to introduce Bertrand to the boys."

While Tru dragged Ducharme off to meet Eddie and Bob, Taryn's gaze skimmed over the room as if she were sizing up the potential of this particular party. She swayed slightly with the soft piano music, her arm brushing against Josh's and sending waves of warmth through his body. He wanted to grab her and hold her still, to stop the torture of her casual touch. He turned his attention to Caroline.

The bride stood on his right, silently observing her guests, smiling and nodding and looking blissfully happy. Tru was lucky to have found such a calm and circumspect woman. Caroline Leighton was definitely not the type to land in jail for destroying a supermarket salad bar. Caroline was a beautiful woman, blessed with all the qualities Josh should want in a wife. Then why the hell did he find himself so attracted to Taryn Wilde?

Josh stiffened his resolve and fixed his eyes on the party guests. He felt as if he were standing in front of a firing squad, nervously awaiting the first shot. His gaze darted back to Taryn, his mind formulating every possible worst case scenario. Taryn punching out the wedding photographer, Taryn starting a food fight with the crab claws, Taryn dancing naked on the—

"Josh, why don't you get Taryn a glass of champagne," Caroline suggested. "The bar is set up on the deck."

"Yes, Josh, I'd just love a glass of champagne," Taryn said, giving his arm an affectionate squeeze. "In fact, bring me two."

With a quelling glare, Josh nodded curtly and picked his way through the room. But by the time he returned just a few minutes later with two flutes of champagne, Taryn was gone. He frantically searched the room as he pressed a glass into Caroline's hand. "Where is she?"

"She's over there," Caroline said, motioning to the small dance floor that had been set up near the piano. "Dancing with Garrett."

His eyes first locked onto her yellow dress, and then Taryn, whirling around the dance floor in his friend's arms. He watched as Garrett whispered something in her ear and she tipped her head back and laughed.

"How long have you and Taryn Wilde been dating?" Caroline asked.

"Since we walked in the door," he replied, his gaze now fixed on McCabe. They were dancing awfully close and having just a little too much fun for people who were strangers only moments before. He stared at them, his attention unwavering.

Caroline waved her hand in front of his face and he turned to her, surprised by the intensity of his concentration. "That long?" she said in mock surprise. "So, when are you two planning to get married?"

"When hell freezes over," Josh murmured. An unfamiliar feeling niggled at the back of his brain. At first, he assumed it was anxiety over Taryn's behavior. But then he realized it was something more. Irritation? No, more like confusion. Suddenly, the feeling coalesced, like a laser beam piercing his consciousness.

He was jealous. Josh bit back a curse then swallowed his glass of champagne in one gulp. What the hell did he have to be jealous of? Garrett was one of his best friends, a man he both liked and admired. And Taryn was nothing more to him than a temporary burden, a debt he owed to a woman he respected. What should he care if they were enjoying each other's company?

"Maybe you should ask her to dance," Caroline suggested.

"What?"

"Go ahead," she urged. "If you don't want her dancing with Garrett, cut in."

"I don't dance," Josh said.

"Don't or won't?"

"Both," he replied. Still, he was tempted to stalk out to the dance floor, to yank her out of Garrett's arms and demand she dance with him . . . causing a scene . . . and displaying the exact behavior he cautioned Taryn against. Josh never, *ever* acted on impulse.

"Then I guess you'll just have to put up with it," Caroline said.

"What do you mean? I certainly don't mind if she dances with Garrett."

Caroline stood on her tiptoes and kissed him on the cheek. "Sure," she said, patting him on the arm. "Whatever you say." With that, she headed back across the room toward Tru, leaving Josh alone with his thoughts.

He spent the rest of the evening on the sidelines, watching Taryn dance with nearly every man in the room. She divided the majority of her time between Garrett and Bert, and in the meantime, downed six glasses of champagne—five more than he had consumed.

At around nine o'clock, to his great relief, the bride and groom bid the party farewell. Gradually the guests made their way to the door. The room was nearly empty when Taryn finally decided to call it a night. She approached him, Garrett on one arm, Ducharme on the other, and Bob Robinson trailing behind.

Her cheeks were flushed with excitement and her eyes sparkled. "There you are!" she cried. "Come on. We're going dancing. Garrett knows of a club that stays open all night."

With deliberate calm, Josh took her by the arm and extracted her from the group. "We're not going dancing," he said.

Her brow knitted in confusion. "If you don't want to come, you don't have to. Garrett will drive us home."

Josh tightened his grip on her elbow and steered her toward the door. "Maybe I didn't make myself clear. *You're* not going dancing."

She tried to pull out of his grasp, but he held firm. Confusion gradually gave way to sheer obstinacy and she dug her heels into the carpet. "You can't tell me what I can and can't do. If I want to go dancing, I'll go."

"No, you won't." His uncompromising reply surprised him. Josh had never considered himself a domineering person, but Taryn Wilde had a knack for unraveling his usually calm approach to matters. There was only one way to deal with her. If he had to, he could be just as stubborn as she could.

She smiled and sneered at him. "Yes, I will."

It was becoming blatantly clear that arguing with Taryn Wilde would get him nowhere. Without another word, he bent over, circled her backside with his arms, and lifted her up onto his shoulder. As he straightened, she kicked out and he grabbed her legs and held them against his chest.

Taryn gasped in shock. "Put me down!" she screeched. "You're making a scene!"

Josh turned to his three friends. They all watched him with barely contained amusement and utter disbelief.

"Josh, what the hell are you doing?" Garrett asked.

Josh ignored the question. "McCabe, make sure Bert gets home in one piece, would you?"

Garrett's eyes widened and he shook his head slowly. "Ah . . . no problem, Josh," he replied hesitantly. "But are you sure you don't need some help . . . escorting Taryn to the car?"

"I think I have the situation well under control, now," Josh replied.

"Don't worry, Josh," Bob added, his voice filled with what sounded like admiration. "We'll take real good care of Bertrand."

With that, Josh nodded, then turned and strode out the front door, a wriggling, enraged harpy tossed over his shoulder like a sack of flour. As he strolled down the sidewalk, he heard Bob and Garrett chuckling behind him, and he smiled to himself. So maybe this was a rather unconventional approach to dealing with Taryn Wilde. But he had to admit—it seemed to be working just fine.

TARYN PUSHED UP, levering her arms against Josh's back. Garrett, Bob and Berti stood in the doorway, watching her humiliating exit. "Don't just stand there," she shrieked. "Aren't you guys going to help me?"

"Sorry, Taryn," Garrett said. "Maybe another time."

"It was nice meeting you, Miss Wilde," Bob added.

"See you later, elevator," Berti called with a wave.

"Cowards!" Taryn yelled. "If you were real men you'd—" Her breath rushed out of her with a *whoof* as Josh began to jog down the sidewalk, his shoulder bumping into her stomach.

"Stop—run—ing," Taryn cried. "I—can't—breathe."

"You also can't yell," Josh said.

"I—promise—to stop," Taryn said.

He slowed down to a walk and Taryn pulled in a deep draught of night air. "Put me down," she demanded.

He bent over and dropped her to her feet, right in front of his car. "You try to run away and I'll catch you," he warned.

She made a move to escape and he trapped her, his hands braced on either side of her shoulders, his fingers splayed against the car. If she didn't know him better, she'd think he was some kind of macho lunatic. But Josh Banks never did anything without careful consideration, including tossing her over his shoulder. Well, she'd show him! She wasn't afraid of him. Still, she'd never seen him look more indomitable than he did at that moment.

Taryn shoved against his arm. "You are despicable. You're nothing but a bully. You can't tell me what to do. I'm an adult and I—"

In one swift motion, his mouth met hers, cutting off her tirade. At first, his kiss was hard and unyielding. Instinctively, she parted her lips, willing him to soften the contact. Then, as suddenly as his lips had ambushed hers, they were gone. Taryn looked up at him, her eyes wide with shock, her heart pounding, self-contempt flooding her senses.

How could she have reacted in such a wanton way? The man had dragged her from the party, from her friends, like some Neanderthal, as if he owned her body. And then he'd kissed her! Well, Taryn Wilde was not about to let any man dominate her in such a way.

"Get in the car," he ordered.

"No!" Taryn replied.

Josh arched a brow, then reached down and yanked the car door open behind her. "Get in now," he said, his voice deceptively calm, "or I'll have to help you in."

She'd never seen Josh so determined—and so angry. And she knew she was no match for him physically. He could easily pick her up and toss her into the car if he chose to. Deciding it was best not to fight him on this point, Taryn grudgingly crawled in and slid across to the passenger seat. Josh followed her and slammed the door behind him. She moved closer to the door and evaluated her chances of escape.

"Don't even try," Josh murmured.

Taryn threw him a petulant glare then stuck out her tongue. Just who the hell did he think he was, telling her what to do, pushing her around like some brainless child?

"Very mature," Josh said.

"Why are you doing this?" she demanded. "I did what you asked. I behaved perfectly at the party."

Josh regarded her skeptically.

"What?" she asked. "I didn't cause any trouble."

He turned his attention back to his driving and Taryn fumed inwardly. What the hell was he getting at? She'd been a perfect guest, quiet and well behaved, even after six glasses of champagne. She'd enjoyed herself, true, but she'd drawn no attention to herself. Taryn glanced over at him and studied his expression. On the surface, he looked furious. But there was more. Realization slowly dawned and she smiled.

"You're jealous!" she cried.

"Don't be ridiculous," he said.

"You are! You're angry because I didn't pay any attention to you at the party. You're upset because I danced with that handsome friend of yours, Garrett."

"I am not jealous," Josh reiterated. "What could I possibly have to be jealous about?"

So stated, the question was puzzling to say the least. Josh Banks couldn't care less about her. To him, she was simply an annoyance, a problem to be dealt with. He had shown her again and again that he was only concerned with protecting Olivia's interests. She was a fool to think there was more behind his motives.

Taryn risked a glance over at him. The passing street lamps painted his face in a stark chiaroscuro, shadow and light playing across potent planes and angles. He was an attractive man, with strong masculine features in perfect balance. Yet, void of emotion, his face was merely ordinary. It was only when anger suffused his expression that his features became so compelling. She wondered what laughter might look like on Josh Banks.

She'd never really seen him laugh. Not the kind of un-inhibited laughter that would move beyond an upturned mouth and a mirthful chuckle. It seemed that Josh Banks didn't allow himself laughter. Instead, he hid his emotions behind a facade of restraint and cool distance.

What had caused him to become the man he was—so strong, yet so silent? He'd only mentioned his childhood once, in passing, when she had commented on the luxury of his office. *I wasn't born with this,* he had said. On the surface, it was an innocuous statement, but the meaning behind it ran much deeper. There was pain in Josh's past, pain that he kept locked up inside of him. Pain that kept him at a distance. And alone.

Taryn pulled in a deep breath, then slowly let it out. If she had but one fear, it was a paralyzing dread of being left alone. Her parents had left her alone. Even when they were alive, she'd still been alone. And later, her grandmother had done the same.

Was it any wonder that she spent most of her adult life collecting people, drawing them into her circle for her own amusement, her own security? Men hadn't been immune to her charms. As time passed, even she had become well aware of her habits. She would lavish her attention on her current *amour* until he was hopelessly besotted, then she would move on to someone else, hoping to find a man who would be worthy of her love. Yet all the while, she kept her love locked tightly inside, terrified to give it to any one person.

Maybe that's what had sent her fleeing Europe and her life there, this growing ability to see inside herself and to hate what she saw. She wanted to love and be loved, she wanted a fulfilling future and a happily-ever-after. But she was also honest enough to know that her past would always play a part in her future, and that true happiness would be impossible to find.

Maybe Josh had been right to drag her away from the reception as he had. In his quest to protect her grandmother's interests, he was also protecting her, steering her away from a life that had become intolerable. Toward the end of her sojourn in Europe, she had tired of the constant demand to be "Taryn the Terrible," to live up to the reputation she had acquired for herself. She had grown to hate the parties, the people, the fawning attention, the incessant chatter.

Though she tried, she couldn't trace her disenchantment back to any one episode. She had simply grown bored with the games, with the artifice, with the expectations. The prospect of maintaining her status as *La Terribile* suddenly seemed overwhelming and frightening. And as determined as she was to leave that life behind, Josh was just as determined to prevent her from going back.

Taryn smiled inwardly. Odd, but when she looked at it from another angle, she and Josh were really on the same side.

The car slowed as it approached Taryn's loft. She watched as Josh searched the street for signs of the photographers. He circled the block three times, just to be sure, before he pulled the car to the curb. Without a word, he got out and came around to Taryn's side, then pulled the door open. He was nothing, if he wasn't well mannered, she mused.

His hand resting protectively in the small of her back, he walked beside her across the street, then shielded her from view as she punched in the security code.

When the lock clicked, she turned and looked up at him. "Thank you for—" she paused "—seeing me home," she finished.

"Open the door," he replied.

She did as she was told and he followed her inside. They climbed the stairwell to the third floor, his hand still splayed above her waist.

When they reached her apartment door, she turned to him again. "Thank you, Josh. For an . . . interesting evening."

"Unlock the door," he said.

She bristled at his intransigent tone. "I really can do the rest on my own," she said. "I'm not a child, even though you choose to treat me like one."

He raised a sardonic brow.

"What? Do you think I'm going to sneak out the back door as soon as you leave?"

His brow rose another few degrees and she felt her temper rise right along with it. Why couldn't he give her just a little credit for common sense and maturity? She wanted to wipe that patronizing smirk right off his mouth. She wanted to . . .

Taryn took a step forward, moving toward him until their bodies were only inches apart. Slowly, she raised her arms and wrapped them around Josh's neck. "I think you're going to have to learn to trust me," she murmured. She pushed herself up on her toes and pressed her mouth to his.

She only meant to return the kiss that he had given her, an impassive meeting of lips. And then she planned to pull away, giving him a good dose of his own medicine. But once her mouth met his, she was lost.

Josh dragged her against his body, his hands spread around her waist, pressing her into his hard chest. This kiss was not rough and demanding, but soft and sensual. His tongue teased at her mouth, urging her to open beneath him. With an inward moan, she did, and their tongues met, sending a jolt of desire through them both.

She pulled back and looked up at him. His eyes were clouded with undeniable hunger. Drawing a deep breath, she smiled tentatively. He moved his hand to her cheek and hesitantly touched her mouth with his thumb. For the first time that evening, she felt as if she were in control of the situation. He wanted her... as much as she wanted him, maybe more.

"Inside," he murmured.

With a triumphant smile, she turned and worked the key into the lock, then pulled the door open. She stepped inside then spun around to face him, blocking his entrance.

"Good night, Warden," she said.

He stared at her, his expression guarded, cautious. "Don't tease me, Taryn," he warned.

"Oh, I'm not," she said, pulling on the door. "It's just that for a moment there, Warden, you forgot who's holding all the cards in this little game." With that, she slid the door shut, then closed her eyes and rested her head against the cool metal.

A long sigh escaped her lips. Even with a steel door between them, it was impossible to deny such an overpowering attraction. Suddenly, she wasn't sure she wanted to.

4

WILDE ONE IN SUPERMARKET SCUFFLE!

The headline grabbed Josh and yanked him to a dead stop as he jogged by the newsstand three blocks from the Bachelor Arms. He stared at the front page of the *Inquisitor*, adjusting his glasses and hoping that he'd misread the inch-high letters. But this time he didn't need a translator to read the latest story of Taryn Wilde's antics.

He hadn't seen her in over a week and had hoped that the uneasy silence from the press, and from Taryn, had meant they had tired of tracking her behavior. Though he'd been tempted to stop and see her, he knew that he would just be asking for trouble.

Josh snatched up a copy of the tabloid and skimmed through the text of the article at a speed-reading pace. Damn, he should have known this was coming. The "melee at the market" was recounted in great detail on the front page and featured a huge photo of Taryn and Ducharme sitting in the back of a squad car.

"Changin' your readin' habits, Josh?"

Josh looked up. "What?" he asked absently.

Vinnie Puccio, the newsstand owner and salesman, stood in the doorway of his storefront bookshop, his trademark unlit cigar jammed in the corner of his mouth. While Vinnie's wife ran the espresso machine inside, Vinnie preferred to spend the mornings chatting with the streetside clientele.

"Usually you go for something a little different. You know, the *Wall Street Journal* or *Business Week*. The scandal sheets ain't exactly the place for financial news."

"I know," Josh said as he flipped through the paper to the second part of the article. "This is personal research." When he finally found the page, his gaze riveted on another photo and he groaned out loud.

There he was. At least there was the back of his head and his right arm, as he escorted Taryn from the Beverly Hills Police Department. His face was obscured from view, but he recognized his navy Brooks Brothers suit and his onyx cuff links.

"Hey, if you like the *Inquisitor*, you should try the *Tattler*," Vinnie suggested, handing him another paper. Josh raced through the *Tattler*'s version of the story, then perused another recommended report by *Inside America*.

Bertrand-Remy Ducharme played the male lead in all three stories and there was much speculation as to the relationship between Taryn and "the handsome French playboy." Though all three articles were gleefully sensationalistic, at least Josh's name hadn't been mentioned. He had been referred to in the captions as Taryn Wilde's attorney, therapist and distant cousin. Beyond those inaccuracies, there were only seven or eight other fictionalizations in each article—including one account that claimed that Taryn was carrying Ducharme's love child.

"How much to buy them all?" Josh asked.

"Three-fifty," Vinnie said.

"I mean, how much to buy every copy you have?" Josh said.

"You wanna buy all my copies?" Vinnie asked.

"Yes." Josh scanned the newsstand, mentally calculating the cost. "What do you have, ten of each?"

"Yeah, that's here on the newsstand. But I got boxes in the back room of the store. These rags sell like hotcakes. We go through at least ten or twenty of each in a day. You can get 'em all over town—gas stations, supermarkets, you name it."

Grinding his teeth, Josh handed Vinnie four dollars, then slipped his wallet back into the pocket of his running shorts. "Never mind," he said. "I'll just take these. Keep the change."

As he walked the three blocks to his apartment building, he reread the articles and closely studied the photos. The photo of him in the *Tattler* was taken from a different angle than the other two and his profile was almost recognizable. Almost, but not quite.

As he stopped in front of the Bachelor Arms and fished around in his pocket for his key, his attention was drawn to an article on aliens infiltrating the CIA. According to the copy, agents had been caught transmitting strange signals into outer space.

"Good morning, Joshua."

Josh glanced over the top of the paper first, then pulled it aside to find Natasha Kuryan standing in front of him. Her sparkling green eyes stared up at him from a diminutive height of just over five feet. Her cheeks were rosy from exertion and a few loose tendrils of white hair had slipped from the tidy knot at her nape.

He often passed Natasha during his morning run as she completed her daily five-mile walk. Often, they would meet at the newsstand and discuss the day's headlines. Spry and quick-witted, Russian-born Natasha was somewhere between sixty and eighty years old, though Josh had never been bold enough to ask her exact age. All he knew was that she was a former makeup artist, had lived at the Bachelor Arms since the end of World War II, and knew everyone that had resided in the building—from the day she had moved in to the present day.

"And since when have you changed your reading habits, Joshua?" she asked, her accent giving an exotic lilt to her words.

"Since this morning," he said. "Vinnie's worried, too." He held out the paper, open to the page with the picture of Taryn, Bert and his obscured profile. "Aliens in the CIA? What do you think?"

"Why, that's you!" she said, pointing to the photo.

Josh blinked in consternation. "You can tell?"

"Darling, I have spent my life looking at faces, from every angle," she replied. "Of course, I can tell it is you. See, here is your nose, so straight and aristocratic. Gregory Peck, he had a nose like this. And your jaw, it is very strong, much like his. Though his lips were too thin. You do not have that problem. But *you* hide your eyes behind those glasses. I have always thought you are a very handsome boy. Good bones, they are the key."

To Natasha, all the male tenants at the Bachelor Arms were "boys." And given another forty years or so, Josh was certain that they all would have been falling over each other for Natasha's favors. Even today, with her hair snow white and her face finely lined with age, she was still a striking beauty.

"So, darling, are you going to tell me what your picture is doing in this nasty paper?"

"It's a long story," Josh said.

"And this Taryn Wilde, she is a friend of yours?"

"No," Josh said, then shook his head. "I mean yes. Sort of." He'd known Taryn Wilde for some time now, and still he couldn't figure out just how to classify their relationship. Baby-sitter came closest. But from the moment he'd tossed her over his shoulder and carried her out of the party, something had changed. A tension had sprung up between them, humming like a live wire, taut and dangerous, ready to snap.

It had snapped the moment he kissed her. At first, he'd only meant to shock her into compliance. But then, she'd softened in his arms and returned the kiss. And when she kissed him again, at her front door, he'd realized that he was not immune to Taryn Wilde's charms.

Had he not had his wits about him, he wouldn't have found the fortitude to stop. It didn't take a rational mind to realize that Taryn preferred to control every situation she faced. Clearly, he wasn't about to gain an advantage on the kissing battlefield. After all, when it came to matters of the lips, she was a four-star general and he, a buck private.

"I worked with Olivia Wilde many times," Natasha continued. "She was a beauty, except for her chin. A bit too long, like a horse, but I fixed that. This girl, she resembles Olivia ... without the chin, of course. She has good bone structure, too."

"She's Olivia's granddaughter. Her father was Oliver Wilde."

"Ah, yes. *There* was a boy born to live up to his name. I remember him, though not fondly. He was arrogant and spoiled. And he had crooked teeth." She smiled wickedly. "But there was nothing that I could do to fix that. Not that I wanted to," she added. "So, are you in love with this Taryn?"

"No!" Josh declared.

"Such a shame," Natasha replied. "The two of you would make lovely babies with beautiful faces."

"No," he restated. "I'm not in love with her. Absolutely not. She's . . . wild and uncontrollable. Loving her would be a . . . nightmare."

Though Josh rarely thought about marriage, he did keep an image of the perfect wife tucked safely away in his subconscious. She'd have to be intelligent and considerate and attractive and affectionate. He tried to recall his mental photograph of Mrs. Josh Banks, but another was blocking its way—an image of pale eyes and rumpled blond hair, a Cupid's bow mouth turned up in a mischievous smile, a soft, sweet body made especially for his hands.

Natasha smiled slyly. "Sometimes, my dear boy, there is a thin line between our nightmares and our dreams, yes?"

"Maybe you're right," Josh murmured.

"Of course I'm right." She climbed the steps to the front door, then placed her finger on a brass plaque beside the door. The name of the apartment building was etched deeply into the metal. "See what this says?"

"Bachelor Arms," Josh read.

"No, scratched into the surface," Natasha said.

Josh pushed his glasses up the bridge of his nose and squinted, then stepped closer. There was something else there. Strange, he'd never noticed the graffiti before. "Believe the legend?"

"Yes, the legend," Natasha said. "That is where it all begins . . . and ends. With the mirror."

"You mean the mirror in Tru Hallihan's apartment?" Josh asked.

"In 1-G, yes. You have seen it?"

"Sure," Josh said. "Lots of times, though not since Tru moved out."

"And what did you see in that mirror?" Natasha asked. "Did you see her?"

Josh watched Natasha warily. "You mean Taryn Wilde?"

"No," Natasha scolded. "The woman."

Apprehension slid down Josh's spine, like a trickle of cold sweat. The breeze suddenly seemed chilly on his skin. He had seen a woman in the mirror, on the day that he'd helped Tru move into 1-G. He'd thought it was just a reflection of someone walking by in the hall, though she was dressed rather oddly. She had smiled at him, but when he turned around, the doorway had been empty.

"What does it mean, when someone sees this woman in the mirror?"

Natasha raised her brows and studied him for a moment, then smiled mysteriously. "Your greatest dream or your deepest fear will soon come to pass." She paused. "So, you have seen her?"

Josh shook his head. "No," he lied. "But I'll keep an eye out and let you know."

"Yes," Natasha said softly, the smile still curling her lips. She took a quick breath, then smoothed a strand of white hair back into the knot. "I must go now," she said brightly. "And so must you. You have many things to discuss with this Taryn Wilde, so I will not keep you." She opened the front door of Bachelor Arms and stepped inside, then disappeared down the hall.

Josh stood, staring after her. Could Natasha have been serious about the legend? Tru must have seen the "ghost." He had mentioned his haunted apartment the other day as they both stood outside Taryn's loft. But Tru's life hadn't changed in any way... except that he had met Caroline Leighton, fallen in love and gotten married. Maybe his greatest dream *had* come true.

Josh glanced back down at his picture in the *Tattler*. He'd seen the "ghost," and now his photo was in three of the nation's biggest tabloid newspapers. He had spent most of the last week trying to figure out how to keep Taryn Wilde from getting into more trouble. And he had spent most of his nights trying to push Taryn Wilde out of his thoughts.

Josh didn't believe ghosts. But if he did, he was certain that Taryn Wilde was not going to turn out to be his greatest dream. No, Taryn had *nightmare* written all over her.

"LOOK AT THIS!" Olivia shouted. "Here she is, plastered all over the *Inquisitor!* You promised to keep an eye on her! How could you let this happen?"

Josh sat in Olivia Wilde's Westwood home, watching the older woman pace around the perimeter of the large living room. He reached for his briefcase and pulled out the other two tabloids. He might as well take his licks all at once. He didn't have the time to answer another summons to appear once Olivia discovered the other photos. "The story made the *Tattler* and *Inside America*, too," Josh said.

Olivia stared at the two papers that he held out, then slowly lowered herself to sit beside him on the couch, the energy draining out of her all at once. "How bad is it?" she asked.

"It's not good," he said. "Most of what you read in the *Inquisitor* was true, and it's repeated in the other papers. She was arrested after she assaulted a photographer in a grocery store. I went down to the police station and bailed her out."

"You got her *out* of jail?" Olivia lamented. "How could you?"

Josh gave her a shocked look and she waved him off.

"Oh, please," she muttered. "I don't want to see her in jail any more than you do, so don't look at me like I'm some wicked old woman."

"You really can't blame her," Josh said. "She was just protecting her privacy. She didn't deserve to be locked up."

"Since when is she interested in privacy?" Olivia asked. "And since when are you taking her side? Her life has been splashed all over the press from the time she was eighteen."

"Maybe she's changed," Josh said. "And maybe you should try to talk to her."

Olivia moaned and leaned back into the cushions, pressing her palms over her eyes. "She will never change, nor will Taryn ever listen to anything I have to say." She coughed weakly.

Josh stifled a smile. He could definitely see where Taryn got her dramatic flair. At one time, he would have jumped to Olivia's aid, but now he suspected that it was just all part of piling on the guilt and getting her own way. He waited a few moments and she peeked out from under her fingers. Finally, she heaved an annoyed sigh and sat up again.

"So, what are you going to do about my granddaughter?" she demanded, rapping him on the arm with a rolled copy of the *Inquisitor*. "The nominations come out in two weeks and, Taryn or no Taryn, my name *is* going to be listed in the supporting actress category."

"I don't know that there is much we *can* do, Miss Wilde. We've offered her money to leave and she's refused. Short of watching her round the clock, I can't keep her from getting mixed up in more trouble. She's an adult, and she'll do what she wants to do."

And she'll do exactly what we *don't* want her to do as well, Josh mused. He had the distinct impression that

Taryn did outrageous things just to enjoy other people's shocked reactions. The more aggravated he and Olivia became, the more she tried to aggravate them.

Olivia's brow furrowed. "But there must be a way. We must think of a plan." She jumped up and began pacing again. Suddenly, she stopped dead and turned to Josh with a beaming smile. "That's it!" she cried.

"What's it?"

"You!"

"Me?"

"*You* will occupy her time."

"With what?" Josh asked.

"I don't know," Olivia scolded, then resumed her pacing. "You think of something. You're young. I'm sure you have common interests."

Josh tried to think of one interest he shared with Taryn, but as hard as he tried, he came up blank. He and Taryn had absolutely nothing in common. At least nothing they had come across. Except maybe, the kiss they'd shared at her front door. They both enjoyed that.

"Maybe you could seduce her," Olivia suggested.

Josh gulped. "What?"

"Well, it's just an idea," Olivia said defensively. "Right now, I'm willing to try anything."

"It's a bad idea," Josh murmured. "Very bad."

"Well, I don't know what to do!" she cried. "Maybe you should try to talk to this French person—this Bernard or whatever his name is. Offer *him* money to take her away. Or what about this other man in the photo? It says here that he's her lawyer. Maybe he could convince her to leave town. We have to try something. We can't just wait for the other shoe to drop."

Josh stood and grasped Olivia's hands, halting her nervous pacing. "Don't worry. I'll take care of it. I suppose I could try to find a way to occupy her time."

Olivia's expression brightened a few hundred watts.

Josh eyed her warily. "But I'd strongly recommend that you just forget that seduction idea."

Olivia scowled. "And I'd recommend that you get started with whatever you have planned for my granddaughter. Today. Now. Before she ends up the subject of another tabloid tell-all."

Josh grabbed his briefcase and started toward the door, Olivia trailing behind him.

"You'll call me and let me know how it's going?" she asked.

He pulled the front door open then turned to her. "You'll be the first to know," Josh said with a resigned smile.

By the time he reached Taryn's loft, he still hadn't formulated a workable plan. Though seduction probably would have been the simplest option, he'd ruled out Olivia's suggestion right away. He'd also ruled out the zoo, Disneyland, and most of the other tourist attractions around Los Angeles. Too many people, too many chances for problems—and photographs. Besides, Taryn didn't seem like the tourist type.

He'd considered taking her to an art gallery or a museum, but knew he'd be out of his element. And knowing her disdain for Olivia, the movies were out of the question, too. It seemed as if the only viable alternative was to stay safely shut up in her loft. But spending the day alone with Taryn would be the worst of all choices. He'd be like a mouse trapped in a room with a cat. Sooner or later, the cat would corner him and he'd be lost.

Maybe it would be best to let her decide. That decision made, he punched in the security code and took the stairs, two at a time. But when he knocked on the door, he realized that letting Taryn decide the day's activities might just get them in *more* trouble. She had turned a simple trip to the grocery store into a fiasco. What would she do with a trip to the planetarium?

The door to her loft slid open and his mind raced for an alternative plan. Someplace quiet, remote, unpopulated. The moon came to mind, as did the summit of Mount McKinley and a deserted island in the Pacific.

"Josh!" Though Taryn's voice and expression hinted at her surprise, her expression was unsmiling. She looked tired, pale, not at all like the Taryn he'd kissed a few nights before. "How did you get in?"

"The door was open," he lied.

"Are you here to pose for me?" she asked bluntly.

"No," Josh replied. "I was—"

"Then go away," Taryn said. "Leave me to my misery."

Josh slowly walked past her to stand inside the loft. "I was just in the neighborhood and I thought I'd stop by." He paused. "And see how you were doing."

"Well, take a good look. I'm not doing well," she snapped. Her hands were covered with paint as was the smock she wore. There were even streaks of blue and red in her blond hair.

"It's all your fault. I'm blocked. I haven't been able to paint anything worthwhile in days."

"My fault?"

"I've been trying to work. Berti's been driving me nuts. And those damn photographers have been hanging around again," she continued, barely pausing for a breath. "Margaux called and informed me that the little brawl at the Food Faire made the front pages of three tabloids. And I haven't been out of the apartment since you dropped me off here three days ago." Her pale eyes watched him suspiciously. "But I guess that would make you and Olivia happy, right?"

"No. Not at all."

She braced her fists on her hips and studied him with narrowed eyes. "Why are you really here? Are you checking up on me? Did Olivia send you?"

"No," Josh replied. "I just thought that maybe you—you might like to come with me."

"Where?"

"To..." He scrambled for something, anything safe and out of the way of tabloid photographers. "The beach. I'm going to the beach and I thought you might like to come with me."

"You're going to the beach, in the middle of a work day, dressed like that?"

Josh looked down at his suit and tie. "I don't plan to go in the water," he said. "I was just going to take a walk." He often played hooky from the office, driving down to the beach and strolling the sand in bare feet and business wear. Other times, he took his morning run there. He loved the serenity and solitude, the time to think, to reflect.

"What is this?" Taryn inquired warily. "Is this some kind of scheme you've cooked up with my grandmother? You're probably planning to toss me out into the surf and hope that I'll drown. Or get eaten by sharks. Or drift off to China."

"I'm simply asking if you'd like to go to the beach," Josh said. "I was planning to go anyway, I just thought you'd like to come along. I thought we might talk."

"Talk?"

He nodded.

"All right," she said, pulling the door closed behind him. "Let me get cleaned up and tell Berti where we're going.

He's in the bedroom watching the Home Shopping Channel. Wait here. I'll just be a minute."

Josh watched Taryn disappear down a hallway, then stepped into the room. Not much had changed since the day they'd met. The large, airy room was still cluttered with canvases, some only half painted. The Chinese screen loomed in the same place in the corner of the room. But as he examined the painting perched on her easel, he realized that something *had* changed.

When he'd first seen her art, he'd brushed it off as foreign and remote, something he'd never appreciate or understand. Now that had changed, for as he looked at the bold swathes of color on canvas, he saw beyond the brilliant blobs of paint. He saw Taryn.

In every daring shape and audacious brush stroke, she spoke. Her story was filled with tumultuous rebellion and hidden sorrow. As if drawn by some magnetic force, he reached out and brushed his finger against the canvas. Like a man blind, he could feel the texture of her emotions beneath his fingertips. It was a powerful recognition.

"Hello, Ward."

At the sound of Ducharme's voice, Josh snatched his hand away from the painting. He slowly turned to find the Frenchman watching him from behind the couch, his arms braced along the back, his expression insolent. Josh nodded. "Hello, Bert."

"Taryn tells me that you have come to take her to the beach."

"That's right. I thought she might like some time away from the loft." And you, his words implied.

Bert's brow quirked up and he wagged his finger. "You know, I see your problem," he said with mock sympathy.

"What problem is that?" Josh asked.

"You are a man between a rock and a cart race."

Josh stifled a smile. "I am?"

"You are in love with her, are you not?"

"In love with her?" Josh said. He forced a casual laugh. Did he have "I Love Taryn" tattooed across his forehead? Where were people getting such a ridiculous idea? First Natasha and now Ducharme. He no more loved Taryn Wilde than he loved a root canal. She was a pain in the—

"Don't bother to deny it," Bert said. "I can see it as plain as Jane. She is not hard to love. But you must know, you cannot take her away from me." The last was a thinly veiled warning.

"I don't know what you're talking about," Josh said.

"Let us put all our cords under the table. Taryn is mine. Maybe she might have enjoyed your caveman behavior the other night, but she will never love you."

Though Josh knew Ducharme's statement might very well be true, he still felt compelled to defend himself. It wasn't that far-fetched that Taryn might find him attractive. After all, she had kissed him. Once. "And why not?"

"Because you cannot give her what she needs."

"And what does she need?"

Bert circled the couch and settled himself on the soft leather cushions. "A place to be herself, a man who loves her for who she is. And, of course, an inheritance of two hundred million francs would not hurt."

"And does she love you?"

"Maybe not now. But, time is on my side. She is almost broke. And when she sees that this artist thing will not work out, she will have no choice but to come back to Europe and her friends, to come back to me."

"You don't think she's a good artist?" Josh asked.

"Look around," Ducharme said. "What do you think? She hasn't painted anything in days."

Josh stared at the painting on the easel, remembering the way the painting had affected him. "Yes, I think she's good. I think she's very good."

"The point is, she does not have to be good. Not if she comes back to Europe with me. She'll will not have to work painting pictures for idiots who know nothing about art."

Josh clenched his fists at his side. He had underestimated Bertrand-Remy Ducharme. He had assumed the man was simply a buffoon. A self-absorbed rich boy with a rather small brain. But Berti was more than that—he was dangerous. He knew Taryn well, he was part of her world. And he also believed that he could make her happy.

A surge of protectiveness rushed through Josh. Ducharme was not the right man for her, he knew it as well as he knew the tax codes. But what the hell was he going to do about it? He was having enough trouble keeping Taryn out of trouble to have time to worry about Berti and his motives. Once, he would have been glad to have Ducharme spirit her back to Europe, but now he knew that the best place for Taryn would be in L.A. With him.

"Maybe she doesn't want to go back to Europe," Josh said.

"We shall see," Ducharme said. "If I were you, I would not count my eggs before they're cracked."

Taryn chose that moment to return, dressed in a gauzy magenta blouse knotted at her midriff and baggy black pants. Bright red toenails peeked out of her sandals and a vivid yellow scarf wound through her hair, shoving it up in spikes and curls. She grabbed her bag and Josh pulled the door open, trying not to appear too satisfied in Ducharme's presence.

"Berti, we'll be back by dinner time," Taryn said. "If you have any problems, call Margaux. Her number is on the memory dial. And please, don't buy anything else. We don't need another porcelain French poodle."

"There is no need for concern," Berti said, pulling himself up from the couch. "I have decided to come with. You know what they say, two's company, three's allowed. Ward doesn't mind if I come along, do you?"

"No," Josh said, fighting back the urge to strangle the guy. "If it's all right with Taryn."

Taryn shrugged. "Why wouldn't it be all right with me? Josh, you go get the car and park down the block. Berti and I will sneak out the back. If we're lucky, we'll avoid the paparazzi."

Ten minutes later, Josh and Taryn were headed west on Santa Monica Boulevard toward the coast, with Berti once again ensconced in the back seat of the Volvo. It became immediately apparent that Ducharme was out to cause trouble—he did not want to go to the beach, he hated the sun, he hated the sand and salt water. He'd simply come along to circumvent Josh's plans for a quiet walk with Taryn. From the time they left the loft, Josh had tried to figure out a tidy way to rid himself of the whining Frenchman. But short of shoving him out the door at the next stop light, there was no alternative. It wasn't until Berti pointed out a billboard for Universal Studios that Josh formulated a plan.

"I think Berti is right," Josh said. "The beach is boring. Maybe we should do something more interesting." He made a quick circle around the block and headed the car in the opposite direction, toward the Hollywood Freeway—and Berti's Waterloo.

A short time later, they pulled up to the front gate at the huge Universal City studio complex, a popular tourist attraction teeming with people. If Josh's plan was going to work, he'd have to play it very cool. To his relief, the lines at the ticket booths were long, the parking areas were packed, and Berti was on unfamiliar turf.

Josh reached into his breast pocket and pulled out his wallet, then turned and handed Ducharme two one-hundred-dollar bills. "Why don't you get in line for tickets? We'll go park the car."

Berti studied Josh carefully, his gaze shrewd. "All right. But Taryn will come with me," he said.

"You wouldn't want to make Taryn stand in line in the hot sun," Josh countered. "The car is air-conditioned. She'd be much better off with me."

"But I would not like her to walk all the way from the parking," Berti said.

"It won't be far. And I need her to help me find a parking spot," Josh said.

Taryn's gaze bounced back and forth between the two of them, her brow furrowed in confusion.

Berti shook his head. "If you cannot find a place to put your car by yourself you are a bigger imbecile than I—"

"Listen," Taryn said. "I don't know where this sudden attack of joint chivalry has come from, but let's make a decision here. Berti, just go get the tickets. Josh and I will find a place to park and we'll join you in line."

For the second time that morning, Josh gave in to a satisfied smile. The Frenchmen fixed him with a glare that could have sliced raw diamonds, then reluctantly crawled out of the car. "Tara, don't let him keep you."

When Berti slammed the door a little more emphatically than needed, Taryn turned to Josh. "What was that all about?" she asked.

Josh shrugged. "Who knows? Must be some French thing." He put the car into gear and pulled away from the curb, leaving Ducharme to stare after them. It wasn't until they turned onto the freeway ramp a few minutes later that Taryn realized something was wrong.

"Where are we going?" Taryn asked.

"To the beach," Josh replied.

She stared at him, her eyes wide with disbelief. "First you toss me over your shoulder and drag me out of a party, and now you kidnap me. I'm getting a little tired of you running my life."

"Live with it," Josh muttered.

"What about poor Berti? You can't just leave him there, waiting for us."

"Bert's a big boy," Josh said. "He can take care of himself."

"But how will he get home?"

"I gave him two hundred dollars. I'm sure he'll figure something out." He turned to her. "But if you really want to, we can go back."

She hesitated, then a smile broke across her face. "No. To tell the truth, he was starting to drive me a little crazy."

"You too? Well then, as old Bert would say, good riddance to bad luggage," Josh said.

Taryn laughed and he turned to see delight suffuse her expression. Lord, she had a wonderful laugh, so free and uninhibited. And a smile that could outshine the sun sparkling on the Pacific. A surge of pleasure shot through him. It was nice to know that he could make her laugh—that he could make anyone laugh for that matter. This time, he'd meant to be funny and it had worked, much to his amazement.

"He's not such a bad guy," Taryn said.

"He's in love with you. And he wants you to return to Europe with him."

Taryn blinked, clearly disconcerted by the sudden shift in conversation. She observed him silently for a long moment. "I know."

Another mile passed before Josh spoke again. "So, what *is* your relationship with him?"

Taryn grinned and shook her head. "You're so polite, so professional. Why don't you ask what you really want to ask?"

"And what is that?"

"What's *really* going on with you and Berti? Where is Berti sleeping? Are you two lovers?"

Josh had to fight the urge to squirm in his seat. "That's not what I wanted to ask," he said, his voice cool. Actually, it was *exactly* what he wanted to ask. But he had no idea how to phrase the question without sounding nosy—or like a jealous suitor. He had absolutely no right to question Taryn's relationship with Ducharme, but that didn't stop him from wanting to know.

Taryn's mouth curled up at the corners. She leaned back against the seat and watched the scenery pass by. "Berti and I are . . . friends. Old friends. Does that answer your question?"

"It'll do," Josh said. For now. But he still had to find a way to rid Taryn of the man's presence. Ducharme was not right for her, no matter how highly the Frenchman rated his chances. Taryn deserved better, she deserved a man who would support her dreams and allow her to grow as an artist.

Not that *he* was that man. Josh knew that he and Taryn weren't compatible. But he couldn't help but want the best for her. He cared about Olivia, and by default, he cared about Taryn, too. Enough to want her to be happy, to be a success. If that meant keeping her in Los Angeles, then maybe he would have to do what he could to keep her from returning to Europe with Ducharme.

What incredible irony! First he wanted her out of L.A., and now he wanted her to stay. If Olivia found out, she'd probably fire him on the spot, past loyalties quickly forgotten. But there *was* one way to control Taryn's behavior, to dilute Berti's influence and ensure her happiness. He just hadn't worked up the courage to play that card. Especially when it required removal of his clothing.

THEY LEFT THE FREEWAY and drove down through the city toward the ocean. As they sped north along the Pacific Coast Highway, Josh made no attempt at small talk and Taryn was content to enjoy the breeze whipping through the open windows of the car. The scenery was glorious, wild and untamed, rock-strewn cliffs tumbling down to roiling surf, divided only by a thin, winding strip of road. She'd been cooped up in the loft for too long and suddenly, she'd been granted her freedom. She wanted to run and shout, tear off her clothes and play in the surf.

They slowly descended from the cliffs until the car reached beach level and Josh pulled into a nearly empty parking lot. He helped Taryn out of the car and continued to hold onto her hand as they made their way out onto the sand. She found herself focusing on the feel of his strong fingers woven through hers. Odd how such a benign contact could make her feel so safe. She'd never really felt that way with any man before.

Zuma Beach stretched before them, nearly deserted on a January weekday, with only a few runners skirting the edge of the water and three die-hard sunbathers who were probably tourists. He had told her the beach was a popular spot for surfers, but the water was almost like glass, with no waves to ride.

Josh sat down in the sand, pulling her down with him. He tugged off his shoes and socks, then stared out at the water. Taryn followed suit, sitting beside him and tucking her knees under her chin. They sat in companionable silence, watching the surf ebb and flow against the smooth sand.

"This is nice," she murmured. "I'm glad you brought me here."

"Umm. Me, too," Josh replied softly.

"What are *you* doing here, Josh?" she asked, staring out at the Pacific.

"I come here a lot," Josh said. "I thought you might like it." He didn't look at her, somehow making it easier for them to speak more intimately.

"No," Taryn replied. "I mean what are you doing in California? You don't seem like the West Coast type. Where do you come from? What brought you here?"

"I came out here after graduate school," Josh explained, "on a pilgrimage. Once I got here, I decided to stay. My family lives outside Chicago. That's where I grew up."

She glanced over at him. "A pilgrimage?"

His smile was sweet but a bit sad. "My father was a huge movie buff. I think he was a frustrated actor. He and I used to spend Saturday afternoons at the movie theater. Just me and him, away from my five sisters and my mom. Most boys play catch or build a tree house with their dads. We went to the movies, every weekend. Westerns, adventures, even musicals, my dad loved them all."

"He must enjoy visiting you out here, among the stars."

His expression suddenly turned remote. "He died when I was twelve."

She placed her hand on his shoulder, wanting to take away some of the pain in his gaze. "I know how hard that must have been for you."

Josh turned to her and nodded. "I tried not to think about how hard it was," he said. "I had to be strong. My mother was devastated and so I tried to take care of things. By the time I started high school, I'd learned to balance the checkbook, pay the bills, and handle the finances. I lived at home while I went to college and when I started graduate school, I had invested enough of my family's money to give my mother and my two younger sisters a good future. She remarried that year." He shrugged and forced a smile. "Suddenly I wasn't the man of the family anymore."

It was as if his words opened a door into his soul. The silent strength that she'd been so fascinated with had been born on the day his father died. He'd given up his childhood to keep his family safe and secure. And when his mother found another man, he'd finally been free to leave and make a life of his own.

"My father died when I was nine," Taryn said. "In a car crash. With my mother. But I'm sure Olivia told you about that."

"Yes," Josh said.

As if it were the most natural thing in the world, he slid his arm around her shoulders. They both stared out at the ocean, as if glancing at each other again might break the trust and openness that had sprung up between them.

"I remember how handsome he was. I used to spend hours just watching him. I'd stand in the shadows while he and my mother threw glamorous parties for all their movie friends. Everybody loved him as much as my mother and I did."

"And did he love your mother?"

"She was his one great love. I often thought the reason he didn't love me was because he didn't have any love left after he gave it all to her. But I wasn't jealous, just resigned to the fact. And happy to be around him."

"You were his daughter. He must have loved you."

"That I was his daughter was an accident of birth," she said with a tight smile. "I don't think they ever planned to have children."

"And what about your grandmother?" Josh asked.

"I *know* she never planned to have me around," Taryn said.

Josh turned to her, his dark eyes penetrating hers. "Taryn, there are a lot of things you don't know about Olivia. A lot she never told you. She's the only family you have left. Doesn't that count for something?"

Taryn dropped her gaze, staring at her paint-stained fingernails. "I don't know. Maybe it does. I'm just not sure." She drew a deep breath. "Can we change the subject? I'd really like to enjoy my afternoon out."

"Sure," Josh said. He levered himself up on his feet then held out his hand. Taryn grabbed it and he pulled her up beside him, then they started down the beach.

Taryn drew in a deep breath of the tangy air. "This really was a good idea," she said. "I can clear my mind here, refocus my energies. Maybe I'll finally be able to paint when I get home."

"Your work isn't going well?"

She sighed. "I don't want to talk about work, either. I just want to enjoy the sun and the sea and forget about all my troubles." Taryn pulled the scarf from her hair and threw it up in the air, then hooted in delight. "I feel like...dancing in the surf!" Suddenly, she felt an overwhelming urge to play in the ocean like a child, to let the waves rush over her, freeing herself of all the troubles she'd experienced in the past few weeks. Taryn tossed her shoes up after her scarf, then began to unknot her blouse.

"What are you doing?" Josh asked.

"I'm going to go swimming," Taryn said breathlessly. "Look at that water. How can you resist?" The blouse slipped off her shoulders and landed behind her in the sand. She reached for the waistband of her pants and Josh grabbed her hand.

"You can't just take your clothes off here," he admonished, his gaze darting up and down the beach.

Taryn glanced around. They were nearly alone. What harm could it do? The only other person near them on the beach was at least one hundred yards away. And it wasn't as if she were going to go in the water naked—though she did prefer to enjoy the ocean that way. "I'm not going to take off *all* my clothes. I know how prudish Americans are about European beach habits. I do have underwear on."

"I don't care," Josh said.

"You're such a prissy old thing," she teased. "Loosen up." She slipped her pants down over her hips then stepped out of them. As she straightened, he grabbed her around the waist and yanked her against him, then turned and shielded her from view of the only other person near them on the beach. She grinned up at him, then wrapped her arms around his neck. "Are you going to come with me?"

Josh bent over and snatched her blouse off the sand. "Put your clothes back on, Taryn," he ordered.

"Don't be such a spoilsport," she teased. "Have some fun." She began to tug at his tie.

Josh pulled the tie out of her hands. "Put your clothes back on now or—"

"Or what?" she challenged.

"Or I'll change my mind about posing for you."

She placed her palms on his hard chest and pushed away. "What are you saying?" she asked.

"You heard me," Josh said. "I've decided to accept your bargain, with certain conditions regarding items of clothing. I'll model for your painting if you keep a low profile. That means no more photos in the tabloids. No more arrests. And no swimming in your underwear."

"When?" she demanded.

"I have to leave town next week for a four-day investment seminar, and if everything goes well, I promise I'll clear my calendar and pose for you when I get back."

Taryn threw her arms around his neck and hugged him. "I can't believe this! This is wonderful." She danced away from him and spun around in a circle, her arms spread wide. For the first time in days, her life had taken a turn for the better. "You won't be sorry," she said. "I promise to stay out of trouble."

"Dammit, Taryn, put your clothes on!"

"Oh, don't come all unglued. After all, you're going to be taking your clothes off in front of me. And I'm going to paint a masterpiece." She stepped back and held out her arms, raising her face to the sun.

"Either you put your clothes on now or our deal is off," Josh warned.

Taryn stuck her lower lip out in a teasing pout then pulled the blouse from his hand. "Someone's got to loosen you up, Josh Banks. You're so stodgy you're in danger of rusting."

He grabbed her pants and held them out to her. "I'm quite loose enough, thank you. Now, I think we'd better get going. It's tax season and I've got a lot of work to do at the office."

"All right," she replied stubbornly. "I suppose I could get started on some sketches. But can't you postpone your trip? I really want to get started now."

"No," Josh replied, trying to keep his tone firm.

As they started up the beach after Taryn had dressed, she glanced over at him. He stared straight ahead. "I'm sorry if I upset your Puritan sensibilities. Sometimes, I just can't control myself."

"Well, you're going to have to learn how."

"Don't you ever feel like just . . . letting go? Forgetting all your inhibitions and allowing your wild side to take over."

"I don't have a wild side," Josh replied.

Taryn slanted a glance in his direction. Though his expression was hard and unyielding, she refused to believe him. Josh Banks definitely had a wild side, somewhere beneath that staid exterior. She'd seen it once. And maybe she was just the person to find it again.

5

WILDE ONE'S MYSTERY LOVER REVEALED!

Taryn stared at the current issue of the *Inquisitor*, her mouth agape. "How can this be? The beach was deserted. There were no photographers there. Who could have taken this picture? We were alone."

"Obviously not," Margaux said, smoothing her chic, short-cropped hair behind her ear. "Who is the man?"

Taryn moaned, clutching the paper to her chest in white-knuckled hands. "This is terrible. This will ruin everything. I'm so sorry, Margaux, I never meant for this to happen. I know this can't be good for business. It's just that they follow me around until—"

"Taryn, please!" Margaux cried, her French accent subtly coloring her voice. She placed a calming hand on Taryn's shoulder. "Don't let this upset you so. This will all be forgotten soon. After you appear on 'Art Exposed,' no one will even remember your time in the tabloids."

"'Art Exposed'?"

"It is a wonderful show on cable television. I have booked you for this Tuesday to talk about your painting. All the collectors tune in. And they do not read these tabloids, so do not worry, *chérie*."

"Tuesday? So soon? Why didn't you tell me about this earlier?"

"Because I did not want you to say no."

"You really think I'll be all right? Nobody really knows me as an artist. And I've never been on television, at least not on purpose."

"You will be just fine. I would not have booked you if I did not think it would help your career. Now, tell me, who is the man?"

Taryn tossed the paper down on the gallery owner's desk and began to wander the room, her mind suddenly focused on her biggest problem. Handling a television interview would be a breeze compared to handling Josh Banks when he caught sight of her latest tabloid appearance.

"He'll be furious," Taryn explained. "I promised I'd stay out of trouble and now this! It's like I've got this big gray thundercloud hovering over my head. Just when I think I can see the sun—BOOM!—it explodes and dumps rain all over my picnic. Maybe he was right. Maybe I should just go back to Europe."

"Do not be ridiculous," Margaux replied. "This is where you belong. Now sit down and take a load off." She pushed Taryn into a guest chair, then leaned back against the edge of the desk and held the paper up in front of her face. "Once more, darling, who is this gorgeous man?"

Taryn forced her gaze to the black-and-white photo and groaned again. There she was, on the beach, in her underwear no less, her arms wrapped around his neck, her lips nearly touching his. Though the photo was slightly unfocused and grainy, both subjects were clearly identifiable. At least the marginal focus made her underwear look like a rather conservative bikini.

She read the caption. "Jet-setting party girl Taryn Wilde romps on the beach with secret lover, L.A. tax accountant Josh Banks." Josh's name reverberated through her head like the sound of a door slamming on her career. He would never pose for her now.

Taryn looked up at Margaux. "Who is he? That's *Male Nude* by brilliant new artist Taryn Wilde," she muttered. "At least, he was going to be *Male Nude* until this picture appeared. Now he's just going to be *Male Mad*. Or probably *Male Furious*. Maybe even *Male Murderous*. I'm doomed."

"Taryn, Taryn, Taryn," Margaux scolded. "You've gotten yourself involved with one of your models? Did I not teach you anything?"

"No!" Taryn cried. "He's not a model. He's my grandmother's tax accountant and financial manager. He's the one I told you about, the one Olivia sent to monitor my behavior while I'm in town."

Margaux's peal of laughter echoed off the high ceiling of the gallery office. She clapped her hands and clucked her tongue. "You are having an affair with your *grandmère*'s tax accountant?"

"No, we're not having an affair," Taryn explained. "I was just fooling around, teasing him. He's just so serious and stuffy and it's so much fun to rattle him. Besides, he'd just agreed to pose for me. I was...grateful." Taryn winced. "I guess this time I went a little too far. I didn't know we were being photographed. This will ruin everything."

When was she going to learn to control her foolish impulses? She had become so accustomed to acting on every emotion, without pause for thought. Could she ever learn to carefully consider every single second of her day? Or would she simply wither under such strict discipline?

It was just an innocent gesture, a teasing hug. Still, as she looked at the photo, she realized that maybe it was more. Even with all his scolding, all his demands, she did enjoy being around Josh Banks. She loved to tease him, to touch him, to watch his gentle, shy smile steal into his serious facade.

"Ah, do not worry, *chérie*. The picture is on page seven, not page one. And there is not even an accompanying story. So, you are involved with a tax accountant. If that doesn't spell *boring* I do not know what does. In another week, they will not want to have anything to do with you."

"That won't make any difference. I made a deal with him. I told him I'd stay out of trouble for a week. In return, he agreed to pose for me when he got back from his business trip." She pointed to his picture. "He is the key, Margaux. Something inside tells me that if I paint him, it will change my life. He's my masterpiece waiting to be put on canvas." She closed her eyes and shook her head dejectedly. "He'll call off our deal the minute he sees this."

"Taryn, he is an accountant. I have got one just like him that you can use," Margaux offered. "He is a bit shorter, maybe, and he has a lot less hair, but he is stuffy enough."

"No, it has to be him," Taryn said. "He has this...silent energy about him. An inner strength and resolve that is so powerful, so seductive."

"Seductive?"

Taryn waved her off. "You know what I mean!"

Margaux gave her a Mona Lisa smile. "I do not think I do understand. Would you like to explain?"

Margaux's implication was absurd. Yes, she had to admit that their kiss the night after the wedding was...intriguing, as was their brief interlude on the beach. But she had also been lucid enough to realize that it meant nothing. After months without a man, she was vulnerable. *Any* man would have triggered the same reaction. She and Josh were polar opposites with absolutely nothing in common and a future that could only be classified as hell on earth. A relationship with him would be folly.

"All right," Taryn acquiesced. "Maybe there was a momentary attraction, but I won't let it go any further."

"Why not?" Margaux asked. "It might do you some good."

"Good?"

"*Chérie*, maybe your creative block has nothing to do with the pressures of your first show, or those photographers, or even your need for a proper model. Maybe it is not what is *in* your life so much as what is *missing* from your life."

"And just what is missing from my life?"

"Passion. That is what makes your work special. Come," Margaux ordered. Grabbing the tabloid with one hand, she held out her other hand and pulled Taryn out of the chair. They slowly walked through the gallery, then stopped in front of one of Taryn's paintings, a huge seascape in oils that Taryn had done two years earlier on Crete. "See," she said. "Passion. This painting seethes with sensuality. The warm water, the dark horizon, undulating waves."

"I painted this right after I broke off my relationship with Alessandro. I was angry."

"But at least you were feeling *something*, darling. Right now, your life, it is empty of passion."

"So, what would you suggest?" Taryn asked. "Do you have a few tubes of passion in your storeroom you might lend me?"

"You need a man. A romance. A fling. What about Berti? Maybe you should lower your standards and get involved with him. He can be quite charming, when he is not an egotistical pig."

"No," Taryn said. "Bertrand-Remy Ducharme is part of a life I've left behind. I'm moving forward now. In fact, I was hoping you might be able to help me with him."

"And what would you like me to do? You know Berti makes me crazy. I only introduced the two of you so he would leave me alone. I don't know how you stand having him around."

"He's all right in small doses. Let him stay with you for a little while. Occupy his time. I can't concentrate with him at the loft. I'm sure if he'd just leave, I'd be able to work."

"All right," Margaux said, waving up her hands in surrender, "send him over. But it will not help. There is only one thing that will get you painting again. A man."

"Just who would you suggest?" Taryn asked.

Margaux held up the paper. "Why not this accountant man?"

"Absolutely not!" Taryn cried. "We would be horrible together. We don't get along. He's so . . . uptight, so demanding."

Margaux raised a brow. "Such a passionate response to such an innocent question, darling."

"Josh Banks is not the solution to my creative block right now, he's the problem. As soon as he sees this paper, I'm going to be out a male model, and you're going to be out a new Wilde series for the gallery opening."

"Darling, you are a very persuasive woman. If you can not get a man to do what you want, then you are not the Taryn Wilde I know so well."

Margaux was right. Taryn Wilde had never needed to work to catch a man's attention. Men had always jumped to do her bidding and she had kept several tightly wound around her little finger at all times. She was certain if she set her mind to it, she could make Josh Banks fall in love with her.

But she didn't want to manipulate his feelings. She wanted his respect. She wanted him to see her as something other than the spoiled party girl she'd been known as for most of her life. And he couldn't do that if she toyed with his emotions.

"Maybe I'm not the woman you've always known, Margaux," she murmured. "Maybe I have changed."

JOSH COULD NEVER SLEEP on airplanes. He'd seen all the old *Airport* movies twice, and though he wasn't afraid of flying, he felt it prudent to remain awake for the entire cross-country flight—even if he hadn't slept in nearly twenty-four hours. The other passengers didn't choose to share his watchful attitude, except for the woman sitting next to him, Mrs. Florence Zabonovich, late of Brooklyn and on her way to live with her daughter and son-in-law in Bakersfield.

Florence, or Flo as she insisted he call her, was a firm believer in the "friendly skies." She had talked nonstop since they'd left the ground at Kennedy. Somewhere over the Great Plains, Josh had feigned sleep, hoping for a little peace and quiet. But he'd gulped down three cups of coffee at the beginning of the flight and now he'd have to give up his nap to answer the call of nature.

The instant he opened his eyes, Florence perked up and started chattering like a hyperactive magpie. Josh quickly excused himself, climbed over her rather considerable bulk and headed for the safety of the lavatory. He stayed inside the tiny cubicle for as long as he could stand it, enjoying the silence, then made his way slowly back down the aisle.

His financial planning seminar had ended on Sunday evening and he'd originally planned to fly back to L.A. on Monday. But after four days and five nights of Taryn Wilde on his mind, he packed, caught a cab and hopped the next flight out. He'd taken the last seat on the 8:00 p.m. flight and was due in L.A. shortly after 11:00 a.m., 3:00 a.m. New York time. Like a transcontinental magnet, she was drawing him back.

The seminar had been a waste of time. During presentations on Keoghs, IRAs and mutual funds, his mind had drifted from the pie charts and bar graphs to an image of Taryn Wilde—stripped down to her black lace bra and bikinis, dancing on the beach, teasing him until he wanted to pull her down into the sand and remove the last scraps of her clothing. Lord, she was beautiful...captivating...irresistible. He envisioned making slow, deep, mind-numbing love to—

Josh swore inwardly. This absurd fascination with Taryn had to stop! It seemed the further he was away from her, the more she plagued his mind. When they were together, she drove him mad with frustration, and when they were apart, he grew distracted with lust. He had a job to do and all it required was keeping Taryn out of trouble. It did not include seduction—mental or otherwise.

"There you are, Joshua!" Florence cried as Josh climbed back into his seat. "For a minute there, I thought you'd fallen in!" She found this vastly amusing, chortling over it until her face was flushed. For a minute there, Josh wished that he *had* fallen in.

Since he'd left his seat, Flo had dragged out her own reading material and she now scanned the front page of the latest issue of the *Inquisitor*. He glanced over and read the headline. To his relief, Taryn's antics had been replaced by a story on a baby born with a face like a frog. Amphibian Baby Born to Shocked Parents!

"Those poor people," Florence lamented. "A baby should be a blessing...not a frog."

Josh opened his mouth, then snapped it shut. But the temptation was too great. "You don't really believe in that stuff, do you?" he asked.

"Oh, yes!" Florence replied. "Look, here's a picture."

"But don't you think that picture could be doctored?"

She stared at the paper, beetle-browed. "Why would they do a thing like that?"

"To sell papers?" At first, this theory brought no rebuttal from Mrs. Zabonovich. She seemed to be intrigued by the possibility. But then, rather than go back to her reading, she decided to argue the point. She began by presenting each article then listing the reasons why it had to be true. By the time she'd reached page seven, Josh was ready to call the flight attendant and ask for nine or ten of those little bottles of bourbon and a very large glass.

"And what about this?" Florence said. "'Wilde One's Mystery Lover Revealed.' I've seen pictures of Taryn Wilde. That's her all right." She held the paper closer. "Hmm. It looks like she's wearing her underwear, doesn't it?"

"What?" Josh snatched the paper out of Florence's hand and stared at the photo.

"See?" Florence said, pointing to the caption. "It says 'Jet-setting party girl Taryn Wilde romps on the beach with secret lover, L.A. tax accountant Josh—'" She looked up at him, her mouth round with surprise. "Didn't you tell me your name was—" She looked back down at the picture, then up at him, blinking owlishly. "This is you! You're Taryn Wilde's secret lover!" Florence reached over Josh and jostled the sleeping woman on his other side. "Can you believe it? We're sitting next to Taryn Wilde's secret lover!" The drowsy passenger opened her eyes, shook her head, then turned back to the window and resumed her nap.

Josh slapped the paper shut, then stuffed it under the seat in front of him, as if that would hide it from the world. "I am not Taryn Wilde's secret lover!" he whispered.

"But that was you, wasn't it?" She didn't wait for an affirmation. "What's wrong? Have you two had a little fight? I've always thought poor Taryn needed a good man in her life. She's an orphan, you know. A terrible tragedy. After she dumped that German baron she was with, I wondered if she'd ever find happiness."

"I believe he was a count. And he was Italian," Josh muttered. He pulled his glasses off and pinched the bridge of his nose. This was just what he needed! Not only had he failed to keep Taryn *out* of the tabloids, he'd managed to get himself *into* them. For all he knew, Olivia had keeled over in her living room already and he'd lost his favorite client. His other clients were most likely combing the Yellow Pages for a new tax accountant. And his five sisters and his mother were probably preparing to fly to California to see what kind of brazen hussy had entrapped their shy, unassuming "Joshie."

Josh glanced at his watch. He had another hour until the plane touched down in Los Angeles. If he hurried, he could get to Taryn's loft before midnight and maybe catch her before she went to bed. They had a lot to discuss. Number one on the agenda would be her reckless behavior on the beach and the resulting photo. Right after that, they'd discuss his tattered professional reputation and their so-called "deal."

He leaned back in his seat and closed his eyes. Florence was still chattering on, now recalling the first time she'd seen Olivia Wilde on screen. Josh drew in a deep breath and attempted to ignore the incessant noise coming from the seat beside him. Slowly, he let his mind drift. The next thing he knew, they'd landed at LAX.

Carrying only his garment bag and the crumpled copy of the *Inquisitor*, Josh found the Volvo in the long-term lot. In minutes, he was on the freeway heading toward Taryn's. A half hour later he was banging on her front door with his fist. After a protracted wait, the steel door finally slid open to reveal Taryn, dressed in a baggy paint-stained T-shirt that nearly reached her knees. Her eyes were cloudy with sleep. Surprisingly, her hair looked neat and tidy for the first time since he'd met her. His frustration dissolved as his gaze took in her disheveled state. She looked so soft, so vulnerable . . . so blameless.

She rubbed her eyes with her fists and squinted at him. "What time is it?"

"Midnight," Josh said.

"Is something wrong?" she asked. Her eyes suddenly cleared then filled with concern. "It's not Olivia, is it?"

"No. Olivia is fine. At least, I think she's fine. Although, I'm not so sure, thanks to you."

"What is that supposed to mean? Josh, why are you here? I thought you were supposed to be in New York."

Josh walked past her, into the apartment, and dropped his bag on the floor. "Where's Bert?" he demanded. He didn't really want to know the answer to that question, especially if the answer was asleep in Taryn's bed. He headed toward the hallway but Taryn's reply stopped him.

"He's staying with Margaux for a few days. What is wrong?"

Josh turned around and pulled the copy of the *Inquisitor* from under his arm. "Have you seen this?"

She didn't bother to look at the paper, she'd obviously seen the photo. She nodded.

"Well, what do you have to say about it?"

Taryn crossed her arms and straightened her spine. "What am I supposed to say?" she said stubbornly. "You don't think this is my fault, do you?"

"You're the one who took your clothes off!" Josh said.

She stalked up to him, fixing him with an angry glare, her eyes suddenly clear and lucid. "Well, I didn't know there was a photographer waiting to take my picture!" She stamped her bare foot on the hardwood floor, then returned to her spot on the other side of the room where she continued to shoot daggers at him with her pale eyes.

"That's no excuse," Josh said calmly.

"What difference does it make?" Taryn said. "It's done. There's nothing you can do about it."

"Our deal's off, Taryn."

Taryn gasped, the sound echoing through the silent apartment. "What? You can't! We made that deal *after* the photographer took the photo. I promised I'd behave from then on, and I have. I've been a perfect angel since you left."

"Perfect angels don't dance around half-naked in public!"

"I didn't know I was being photographed!" she yelled. "It's not my fault."

"He wouldn't have taken your picture—or mine for that matter—if you'd kept your clothes on."

Her brow furrowed and she crossed her arms. "Is *that* what's bothering you? That *you're* in the picture?" She studied his face with a keen gaze. "This isn't about Olivia or her damn award or my behavior. This is about you!"

"I don't particularly care to have my picture featured in one of these papers," Josh said. "I've got a business reputation to maintain."

"Oh, I'm so sorry," Taryn said with sarcastic sympathy, crossing the room again, coming toe-to-toe with him.

"I'm sorry that associating with me would cause such harm to your precious reputation!"

"That's not what I meant," Josh said.

"I know exactly what you meant," she said. "You're just like Olivia. Taryn is trouble, plain and simple. Send her away, far away! Out of sight, out of mind. She can't harm your career from another continent."

"Taryn, I—"

"Is that what you want? Do you want me to leave?"

Josh grabbed her by the arms and pulled her against his body. "No! I don't want you to leave."

"Then what do you want?" she said, her jaw tight with anger.

Josh looked down into her stormy gray eyes. At that instant, all he knew was that he didn't want to talk anymore. With infinite patience, he lowered his head, pausing for a long moment, his lips nearly touching hers, waiting for a sign. She froze, her warm breath teasing at his mouth. Then, ever so slowly, she moved forward until their lips touched.

With a groan, he covered her mouth. Her body molded along his, warm and pliant, her breasts pressed against his chest. Josh brought his hands up to her face, weaving his fingers through her short, silky hair and slanting her mouth against his. She felt incredible in his arms, as if their bodies were made for each other.

As he deepened the kiss, his tongue teasing at hers, he slowly skimmed his hands down along her arms, savoring the silken skin beneath his fingers. He felt an undeniable compulsion to touch all of her, every perfect inch of her body, until he knew her by heart.

He teased at her lower lip with his teeth, then drew a line of soft kisses along her jaw to her ear. Josh slipped his hands beneath the bottom of her T-shirt and slowly traced a path with his palms along the outside of her thighs to her hips. He stopped there for a moment, drawing a sharp breath, when he realized she wore no underwear. Somehow, he knew that Taryn slept naked, that the T-shirt was tugged on before she opened the door for propriety's sake. His blood heated another few degrees.

A hazy image slipped though his mind...Taryn asleep, a bare leg twisted in the bedclothes, a perfect breast peeking from beneath the sheets. He imagined himself pulling the sheet back, exposing her body to his gaze. And as the image danced in his mind, his hands moved again, along her slender waist and rib cage until his thumbs stopped against the soft underside of her breasts.

She was so tiny, so flawless, as if she'd been made for his touch. Pushing up on her tiptoes, she kissed him, and this time she was more aggressive, moving against his hands, brushing along the hard ridge of his desire.

Her hands spread his jacket open, skimming over his shirt and stopping to work his tie loose. She managed three buttons on his shirt before she gave up in impatience and turned her attention back to his mouth. This was the Taryn he wanted, bold, determined, a woman who would settle for nothing less than his best. A woman who would never cease to fascinate and puzzle him. As he wanted to learn her body, he also wanted to explore her mind. What made Taryn Wilde tick?

Josh pulled back and looked into her upturned face—the sooty lashes against pale skin, the rosy flush that suffused her cheeks, the satisfied smile that curved the corners of her mouth. What was it he felt with this woman? What power did she have over him? Against all common sense and self-preservation, he realized he was falling in love with her.

"Are you still angry with me?" she murmured, opening her eyes to meet his gaze.

He shook his head and smiled. "I'm sorry," he whispered. "I know it's not your fault. You didn't know the photographer was there."

"What made you so angry then?"

"I—I feel like that photographer spoiled something between us," he murmured, his gaze trapped by hers. "Something private."

She placed her palm on his cheek and he turned and placed a kiss in the center. "It's just a stupid picture," she said. "It's not true what they say. You're not my lover."

"But I could be," Josh said.

Taryn looked at him with wide eyes.

"I—I didn't mean that the way it sounded," Josh said.

"You didn't?" Taryn said breathlessly.

"No. What I meant was, I could be your lover . . . if you wanted me to."

A frown creased her brow. "I—I don't know. Maybe I do."

"What does that mean—maybe?" he asked.

She stepped away. "It means maybe. It means for once, maybe I'd better look before I leap."

"You picked a fine time to change your ways," Josh said hesitantly, trying to lighten the mood. He slowly reached out and captured her chin with his fingers, then kissed her, long and deep. In an instant, his desire flamed hotter and he wanted her, more than he had wanted any other woman in his lifetime.

But Taryn didn't feel the same. She pushed against his chest and took another step back. Doubt troubled her gaze and Josh moaned inwardly. "Maybe you're right," he conceded, calming his raging hormones. "Maybe we better think about this for a minute."

"Yes," Taryn said. "I think that would be best. If we do this, we might regret it later."

"Or we might not," Josh said.

Taryn pulled out of his embrace and paced in front of him, twisting the hem of her T-shirt nervously. "We're just so different. I don't know if this . . . step is wise."

"We are different," Josh agreed. "But that's not necessarily bad."

"I'm an artist, you're an accountant. You're stuffy and straitlaced. You're too conservative and too dictatorial."

"And you're reckless and undisciplined," Josh returned.

"You're right, we better consider this carefully," Taryn said. "We'd probably kill each other before long. And I don't want that to happen, Josh."

Josh grasped her shoulders and halted her pacing. "So, where does this leave us, Taryn?"

"I don't know," she said. "But I don't think I can decide now. I'm too . . . distracted."

Josh sighed, forcing his mind away from the tantalizing image of her naked body beneath the T-shirt. Finally, he smiled, then kissed her on the forehead. "Whatever you decide, I want you to know that I care about you, Taryn. I want you to believe that. This isn't all just about Olivia."

Taryn nodded. "I think I know that. Now. Maybe you'd better get home. You look like you could use some sleep. And I've got a big week ahead of me. Margaux's booked me on a television show on Tuesday."

"A television show?"

"'Art Exposed.' I'm going to talk about my work. I'm really a little nervous. No one has ever interviewed me about my art before."

"Would you like me to come with you?" Josh asked.

She gave him a wary look. "Why would you want to come? To make sure I behave?"

"No, for moral support. It might help to have a friend there."

Taryn smiled gratefully. "You'd do that for me?"

"If I'm going to model for you, I guess I better familiarize myself with the business."

Taryn threw her arms around his neck and pressed a kiss against his mouth. "I'm going to be too nervous to get any painting done tomorrow. We'll start bright and early on Wednesday morning. I'll need to do some sketches first. But maybe I can be painting again by the weekend."

"Then I'll see you on Tuesday," Josh said.

"Tuesday," she repeated.

Josh walked to the door and she trailed after him, and pulled the door open. Her cheeks were flushed with excitement and her eyes sparkled. He gave her a quick kiss then chucked her under the chin. "Behave yourself," he said.

She grinned at him as she pushed him out the door and slid it shut behind him. And like the effect of a sudden brilliant light on the eyes, her smile stayed with him all the way home.

FLYNN'S WAS STILL OPEN by the time Josh pulled into his parking spot at the Bachelor Arms. Though he was dead tired and hadn't slept in nearly twenty-four hours, he knew that he wouldn't be sleeping much that night either, not with Taryn Wilde teasing at his dreams. Maybe a bourbon would help.

To his surprise, Garrett McCabe and Bob Robinson were sitting at the end of the bar. He ran his fingers through his hair and straightened his jacket, then walked over to them and took a place on the stool next to Garrett.

"Hey there, Josh!" Garrett said. "What are you doing here?" Garrett raised his hand. "Eddie, get Josh a drink. Geez, Banks, you look like hell. What did you do, sleep in that suit?"

"Almost," Josh murmured. "But not quite."

Eddie placed a bourbon on the rocks in front of Josh. Josh picked up the glass and downed the drink in two swallows then motioned for another.

"You're usually not out this late on a Sunday night," Eddie commented. "Were you at the office?"

"I just got back from New York. Investment seminar. I got in a few hours ago."

Garrett took in Josh's rumpled appearance and grinned. "Did you ride on the wing?" he teased. "I've never seen you looking so scruffy."

Josh glanced down and realized that the top three buttons of his shirt were still undone. "It was a long flight."

"Hmm." Garrett nodded slowly. "So life's been tough lately, huh?"

Josh glanced over at his friend and watched a grin quirk his mouth. "What?"

Garrett pushed a small piece of paper across the bar with his index finger. "Recognize the guy in the photo?"

Josh didn't even have to look at the clipping to know what it was. Ah, the power of the press. He wondered if there was *anyone* who hadn't seen the damn photo.

"I was telling Eddie and Bob that they probably took a picture of your head and pasted it on some other guy's shoulders," Garrett explained. "'Cause that couldn't possibly be our Josh cavorting on the beach with Taryn the Terrible. The last time we heard, you were keeping her out of trouble, not getting her into it."

"I'd say it's more like the other way around," Josh said.

"That's my kind of trouble," Garrett said. "So, how does it feel to be a tabloid star?"

"Not great," Josh replied. "This isn't going to be good for business."

"It may not be good for business, buddy, but it'll do great things for your personal reputation. The ladies will be impressed."

Josh shook his head then pulled his glasses off and rubbed his eyes. "I don't know how this got so out of hand," Josh said. "When I went to see her that first time I actually thought she'd just scurry back to Europe with a bigger bank account. But she is, by far, the most exasperating woman I've ever met. She won't do anything I say. Put my five sisters together, multiply that by fifty and they don't even come close to Taryn."

"That's a dangerous kind of woman you're dealing with there, Josh," Garrett said.

Josh nodded and silently sipped at his second drink.

Bob picked up the clipping and scrutinized the photo. "She's just a little bitty thing," Bob said. "She doesn't look dangerous to me." He tossed the photo down and pushed away from the bar, then bid everyone good-night.

Josh watched him leave then turned back to Eddie and Garrett with a frown. "Where did I get the idea that Bob lived here? Doesn't he sleep in that chair?"

Garrett's shout of laughter startled Josh. "And where did I get the idea that you didn't have a sense of humor?" Garrett asked.

"I didn't," Josh admitted. "I think I'm developing one as a result of being around Taryn Wilde. A guy's got to have a sense of humor to spend much time with her, or he'll turn into a raving lunatic."

"Just how bad is it?" Garrett asked.

Josh shrugged. "I guess most of my clients will realize that I—"

"That's not what I meant, Banks," Garrett said. "I meant how bad have you got it for Taryn Wilde?"

"Got what?"

"Got the hots."

"The hots?" Josh rubbed his face with his hands then sighed. "I don't know. I'm not sure. She's just not what I expected."

"What did you expect?"

"I expected that I'd meet a woman someday and I'd get married and we'd have a regular life." He paused. "Taryn's not that woman, but that doesn't seem to stop me. How do you do it, McCabe?"

"Avoid marriage?" Garrett said.

"Not just that. How do you avoid falling in love? Especially with the wrong kind of woman."

Garrett paused. "I guess some of us just are meant to be happily unmarried. I've just never found a woman I'd be interested in spending the rest of my life with."

"But the crazy thing is, there are moments when I *can* imagine spending the rest of my life with Taryn Wilde," Josh said. "I can imagine bailing her out of jail every few months. I can imagine watching as she rips off her clothes at the slightest provocation. I can even imagine beating off all her old boyfriends with a stick. And even though this sounds kind of sick, I think I'd actually be happy with her."

Garrett clapped him on the shoulder. "You're delusional. It's jet lag. We better get you home to bed before you start picking out crystal and china and talking about your lawn. Believe me, you'll get over this."

"I hope so," Josh said. "Lately, I just haven't been myself. I can't figure it out."

Garrett stared at him for a long moment, his brow creased with concern. Then he sighed and shook his head. "Maybe she's the one," he said.

"The one?" Josh asked. "What one?"

"*The* one," Garrett said. "Just give yourself time, Josh. Don't jump into this headfirst. The water might only be a few inches deep and you might get hurt."

"Water?" Josh asked, thoroughly confused by the turn in the conversation.

Garrett nodded. "I didn't always take my time. But after smashing my head on the bottom of too many shallow relationships, I've given up diving. I prefer to sit around the pool and enjoy the scenery. I'm waiting for a deeper pool. Know what I mean?"

Josh frowned. "Not really."

"I date a lot of women and that's as far as it goes," Garrett whispered.

"That's it?"

"Reputation isn't always reality," Garrett said. "And I'd appreciate if you'd keep that a secret. My readers have been led to believe I live a rather exciting life."

Josh swallowed the rest of his drink then stood up. "Reputation isn't always reality," he repeated. "Got it."

The theory didn't only apply to Garrett. What kind of woman would he find beneath Taryn Wilde's reputation? Was she really the irrepressible party girl that the press seemed determined to perpetuate? Or was she simply a headstrong woman trying to make her dreams come true?

Whichever woman was hiding beneath the public facade, he knew, against every shred of common sense he possessed, he was falling in love with her. And there wasn't a damn thing he could do about it.

6

"GOOD EVENING. It's Tuesday and it's time for 'Art Exposed.' I'm your host Elsa McMillan."

Taryn folded her hands in her lap and glanced nervously over at the television monitor. To her alarm, she found herself looking directly at her own image. She quickly looked away and tried to compose herself, embarrassed by her naive blunder.

She'd never appeared on television before, much less discussed her work in public. Though the rather spooky-looking Elsa had run down a list of questions she planned to ask, Taryn still felt a bit uneasy. This show was an opportunity to showcase herself as an artist and to get some good publicity for the opening. She just couldn't be caught looking dim-witted on cable television.

The show was broadcast live without an audience from a small Beverly Hills community access studio. The studio was empty, except for the guests and the host on stage. But somewhere in the dark, Josh stood, watching her. He'd driven her to the studio, calmed her nerves and waited with her in the wings until it was time for her to take her place on the set.

Taryn drew a slow, steady breath. If art collectors were going to take her seriously, she would have to show absolute confidence in her work. She felt better knowing Josh was there. He seemed to have confidence enough for both of them. At first she had worried about seeing him again, wondering how they'd relate to each other after they'd nearly tumbled into bed two nights before. But Josh seemed to sense her apprehension, and he didn't bring it up. Right now, she was glad to have his strength and assurance, rather than torrid images of his lovemaking racing through her mind.

Since their passionate interlude, they had seemed to settle into a tenuous friendship with each one learning to respect the other's idiosyncrasies. He'd stopped by the loft on Monday and Tuesday morning, just to check in, and had taken her to dinner Monday evening. He seemed relaxed in her presence, almost trusting, and she sensed that Josh was becoming more tolerant of her unconventional approach to life. And at the same time, she was coming to admire his solid strength and conviction.

"Tonight, we have a very interesting show for you," Elsa intoned in her nasally voice. "With us is Taryn Wilde. Ms. Wilde is a member of one of Hollywood's royal families and a promising new painter. She is scheduled for a showing at the Talbot Gallery in mid-April."

Certain the camera was still on her, Taryn forced a smile and nodded at the host. Elsa was a dour-looking woman of indeterminate age. She wore her waist-length black hair parted down the middle and pulled forward over her shoulders, magnifying her pale face and her stick-thin body. Her rumpled clothing matched her dyed hair. Elsa didn't bother with a reassuring smile, she just turned to her next guest and introduced him in her pedantic drone.

"Also with us tonight is Data Rewind. Mr. Rewind is one of L.A.'s most intriguing performance artists and currently has a show at Theater X. Data will talk to us about his piece, *The Monkey Diaries*."

Data was a tall, gangly young man with a crew cut and huge black-framed glasses. Either he'd changed his name or Mother Rewind had been particularly clairvoyant at his birth. He looked exactly like a "Data." He, too, was dressed completely in black. Taryn glanced down at her striped top, her wildly patterned skirt and her tribal jewelry. Maybe she'd made a mistake in her wardrobe, but she loved bold, outrageous colors and interesting textures. Though she wore black on occasion, she found it a little boring and pretentious on a daily schedule. And virtually lifeless on camera. After all, she wanted to be noticed, didn't she?

The third guest sat on the other side of Elsa and was dressed in a conservative suit. Taryn didn't recognize him, but then again, she wasn't yet familiar with the L.A. art scene. The gentleman had three canvases propped up against the side of his chair. She hadn't bothered to question the producer about the other guests, but assumed the man was probably a gallery owner or a museum curator by his lofty expression. Even so, the man reminded her of a turtle. His tiny, balding head was perched atop an enormous bulk of a body and his beady eyes were sharp and a bit cruel. His short little arms barely reached around his girth and linked in his nonexistent lap.

"And finally, I'd like to introduce Mr. Edwin St. Andrews. Mr. St. Andrews is a nationally recognized art critic and is currently on staff at the *Los Angeles Post*."

Taryn sucked in a sharp breath and her heart dropped in her chest. Oh, God, she was on the same stage as Edwin the Executioner. She'd heard Margaux rant and rave about the critic, claiming he could make or break an artist with just one word—or the lack of one word. St. Andrews had dubbed one of Margaux's discoveries "charmingly predictable" and the showing had been an unqualified disaster. Another he'd ignored completely and the artist became instantly invisible to collectors. "Hack" and "amateur" didn't even enter his vocabulary. Edwin St.

Andrews hid his poison arrows behind clever, erudite phrases.

"Why don't we begin tonight's discussion with Ms. Wilde," Elsa said.

"Yes," Edwin said. "Why don't we?" His voice dripped with condescension, magnified by his snooty British accent. A smirk settled on his fleshy lips. The haughty look he sent her chilled her to the bone. Less than a minute into the show and Edwin St. Andrews had found a target for the day. He was lining Taryn up in his sights.

Taryn drew a deep breath. She could handle this man. Hey, Taryn Wilde could handle *any* man. She was an intelligent, competent woman and whatever ammunition he chose to use, she could deflect it with grace and good taste.

"Tell us about your background, Ms. Wilde."

"Well, Elsa, I began painting when I was quite young and I—"

"A pity someone didn't stop you while you were ahead," Edwin quipped.

Elsa smirked in malicious enjoyment. She had obviously decided not to censor Edwin's commentary. Even Elsa didn't want to get on the man's bad side, though Taryn wondered if a man they called "The Executioner" bothered with a *good* side.

Taryn smiled at Edwin as if he'd made a clever joke. "Actually, I did stop painting for a while, after my parents died. But then I was convinced to pick up the brush again by a good friend. Her name is—"

"Oh, yes, please do give us a name. We'll have the culprit arrested and flogged."

Taryn snapped her mouth shut. She wasn't about to give Edwin the opportunity to shred Margaux's reputation as well. Data Rewind shot her a sympathetic but equally terrified look from behind his enormous glasses. Edwin St.

Andrews was in rare form this evening and it was clear Data sensed he'd be next on Edwin's hit list. Elsa simply watched the whole scene with a mercenary gleam in her eye. Obviously, this type of rude behavior was welcomed on "Art Exposed" and she would do nothing to stop it.

"I spent a year in Paris," Taryn continued after a marked pause. "While I was there I studied with Henri Lescault. He encouraged me to pursue my art."

"A fine house painter with a keen eye for color," Edwin said.

Taryn's confidence fell. Why had he chosen to attack her this way? She'd never even met the man. And she doubted that he'd ever seen her work. Taryn schooled her temper and stiffened her resolve. She could deal with this boor if she just maintained her cool. "Actually, Henri taught at the Sorbonne. He was a well-respected painter and quite influential in my early career."

"If he was so influential," Edwin sneered, "why didn't he—"

"Enough!" The command came out of nowhere, echoing through the studio like a sonic boom. Elsa jumped in her chair while Data frantically looked for the fastest escape route. Edwin chose to hold further comment, while Taryn squinted out into the studio, praying that the voice hadn't come from Josh.

But as Josh materialized out of the dark, a thunderous expression on his face, Taryn knew her prayers would not be answered. "Stop the tape," Josh ordered.

"I'm afraid we're broadcasting live," Elsa said with a condescending tone. "But, please, feel free to enlighten us on your opinions about Ms. Wilde's painting."

"Josh, please," Taryn pleaded.

"Taryn, you don't have to take this," Josh said, his jaw tense. "Come on, let's go. I'm taking you home."

She lowered her voice. "This is *live* television, Josh. I can't just leave."

"Then turn off the damn cameras," he demanded. "I will not sit here and listen to this overblown windbag insult you or your work."

"She'd better learn to take it," Edwin said, pulling his enormous bulk from his chair. "If her work is anything like—"

Josh pointed at Edwin, his finger sending a clear warning. "Don't say another word, tubby!" he ground out. "You are nothing but a self-absorbed, egotistical garden slug. A slug that knows nothing about art. Taryn is a brilliant painter."

Elsa stifled a harsh laugh and covered her lividly red lips with her fingertips.

"And you, sir, are an ill-bred knave who wouldn't recognize good art if it bit you in the—"

Edwin's last word never made it out of his mouth. In three long strides, Josh crossed the stage, picked up one of the canvases beside Edwin's chair, and smashed it over his shiny, little head. Edwin sputtered in surprise and his complexion turned apoplectic. Elsa gasped in shock. And Data just moaned and slumped down in his chair. Before Edwin could hurl another insult, Josh pulled the painting up and over the critic's shocked expression and held it out to the camera.

Josh looked at it critically. "This *is* good art," he said, pointing to the hole in the canvas.

It didn't take long for Edwin to find his voice. "You— you hooligan! You ruffian! I'll see you thrown in jail for this. Elsa, call the authorities. I want this man arrested!"

"Right," Josh said, tossing the ruined painting aside. "And while they're at it, they should arrest you."

"For what, pray tell," Edwin sneered.

"For impersonating a human being," Josh said.

That said, Elsa waved her hand until the camera swung back to her. "We'll continue our spirited discussion after this word from our sponsor," Elsa said.

"We don't have any words from our sponsors," the floor director hissed. "We're commercial-free."

"Then turn the damn cameras off," Elsa screeched. "Now!"

"And we're out!" the floor director said. The cameramen stepped away from their cameras. Elsa gently drew Edwin back to his seat. Data stifled a tiny moan and continued to chew his fingernails. And Taryn looked up at Josh and shook her head.

Her career as an artist was over.

"HOW COULD YOU?" Taryn cried.

Josh looked up at her. How could he? Good question. He was trying to figure that same thing out himself. What the hell had possessed him to bash Edwin St. Andrews over the head with a painting? It was like some jungle instinct took over, Tarzan swinging in to protect his Jane.

Josh shook his head. For the second time since he met Taryn Wilde, he watched her through the bars of a Beverly Hills jail cell. Only this time, *he* was on the wrong side of the door. True to his word, Edwin St. Andrews had prevailed upon the authorities to put that "uncivilized hooligan" behind bars. The show had continued on without Taryn and St. Andrews, and now that the program was finally over, Josh waited for the police to finish interviewing Elsa and Data Rewind.

Never in his life had he done something so impulsive, so ill-advised. He'd always had invincible control over his emotions and his behavior. He sat down on the hard cot and rubbed his forehead, then looked up at Taryn. Maybe

he'd been spending too much time with her. Her reckless-
ness was beginning to rub off on him!

But what other choice did he have? The man had been
roasting Taryn alive, insulting her, belittling her work
until Josh had no choice but to stop him. His need to protect Taryn had been overwhelming and he'd taken the first
course of action that had come to mind. Edwin St. Andrews deserved exactly what he got. Josh just regretted
that he had been the one to mete out the punishment.

Taryn clutched the bars and glared at him. "Do you
know what this will do to my career? Edwin St. Andrews
is the most important art critic in Los Angeles, on the entire West Coast for that matter. He can make or break me
with just a few well-aimed words."

"The guy is a pompous jerk," Josh muttered. "Didn't
you hear the way he was talking to you?"

She pushed away from the bars with a frustrated groan.
"That's just the way Edwin acts. It's all part of his per-
sona."

"Well, I didn't like it," Josh said.

"*You* didn't like it," she mocked. "So, *you* hit him over
the head with that painting? That was completely un-
called for. I was handling him."

"Handling him? You were letting him insult you left and
right. I was just watching out for you."

"I don't need you to watch out for me!" Taryn shouted.
"Edwin has trashed some of the best artists in this country. If he thought I was that bad, he wouldn't have bothered tearing me to shreds on live television."

Josh stared at her, completely befuddled by her reason-
ing. He scrubbed at his face and then looked at her again,
his brow furrowed. "That makes absolutely no sense at
all," he said.

"Well, maybe you're just going to have to accept the fact that you know nothing about the art world," Taryn said.

He watched her as she paced back and forth in front of the cell door. After all this, he just wanted to take her into his arms and smooth away the tension that hid her lovely face. "I know your work is good," he said. "And I know it's about time someone stuck a pin in that overinflated windbag you call an art critic."

"And you think this will do it? Josh, he will never give me a good review now. He'll find any excuse to destroy me. And ruin my career at the same time. Edwin is like an elephant. He never forgets. This little incident will live on in infamy and my name will be linked with this embarrassment for as long as I paint or as long as I live, whichever comes first. All my appearances in the tabloids don't add up to this mess you've made."

"Taryn, anyone who watched that show will have to sympathize with you."

She stamped her foot petulantly. "They won't care. They're the ones who listen to Edwin. Besides, I've already got two strikes against me. I'm not a formally trained artist and my last name is Wilde. Edwin's wrath just makes strike three."

Taryn rested her forehead on the bars, her eyes moist, her bottom lip trembling. Her defeated expression was like a knife to his heart. Taryn was so resilient, so unflappable, nothing ever rattled her. But she looked utterly vulnerable, as if some secret anxiety had been exposed to the world. He knew she was uncertain about her future, insecure about her artistic talents, but he hadn't realized these things lived so near the surface. Suddenly he regretted his actions for a different reason—for the pain that they caused her.

He stood and crossed the cell, then covered her clenched hands with his. "I—I'm sorry, Taryn. I was only trying to protect you. Please don't cry."

"I'm not crying," Taryn muttered, wiping at her nose. "And don't try to rationalize your behavior. I remember the verbal thrashing you gave me after my little scuffle in the supermarket. And I was only trying to protect my privacy."

"I understand that now," Josh said.

She sniffled. "I wonder what Olivia will have to say about this?"

"Oh, no," Josh groaned. "Olivia. They announce the nominations tomorrow, you know. She won't be pleased by this."

Taryn patted him on the hand. "Don't worry," she said tartly. "She'll probably find a way to blame this whole mess on me."

At that moment, an officer walked into the cell block and stopped at Josh's cell. Taryn recognized him from the supermarket brawl. He looked at them both, then frowned. "Have I seen you two before? Do I know you?"

"No," they both said simultaneously.

"Really? I could swear..." He shrugged and shook his head. "We've talked to Ms. McMillan, Mr. Rewind and the two cameramen. There seems to be a general agreement that Edwin made some deliberately provoking comments. He's agreed to drop all the charges in return for an on-air apology. And you'll have to reimburse him for the value of the painting."

"Don't do it," Taryn said. "Don't apologize to that slimeball."

"Tell Mr. St. Andrews that I would be happy to apologize to him. And I'll write him a check for the painting. How much was it?"

"Fifty," the police officer replied.

"Fifty thousand?" Josh asked, his voice choked. Good Lord, Taryn was right. He knew absolutely nothing about art. How could a little painting like the one he smashed over that slug's head be worth fifty thousand dollars? He'd seen paintings exactly like it being sold on the side of the road for twenty or thirty dollars.

Taryn gave him a long-suffering look. "Oh, please," she said. "That painting was pure kitsch."

"She's right," the police officer said. "Mr. St. Andrews said it was by some guy named Kitsch. He called it couch art, but from what I could see it wasn't a picture of a couch. It was trees and a lake. I got one just like it in my living room."

"So, how much?" Josh demanded.

"Fifty. Fifty dollars," the policeman said.

Josh sighed in relief. So he wouldn't have to declare Chapter 11 to pay for a wrecked painting. "I guess I should be glad Mr. Kitsch isn't much of an artist," he muttered.

"Josh, there is no Mr. Kitsch. Kitsch is just a word used for bad art. You know, Elvis on velvet, dogs playing poker, wide-eyed waifs."

Josh stared at her blankly then turned back to the officer. "Fine. Fifty dollars and a public apology. Just unlock the door and give me my checkbook. We'll take care of this right away."

"I can't believe you're going to apologize to that creep," Taryn complained.

The door swung open and Josh stepped out, then grabbed Taryn's arm and steered her toward the exit. "There are times when it's best to cut your losses and run," he whispered. "I don't want to spend the night in jail."

"You were going to let me spend the night in jail not too long ago."

"Taryn, you don't need to remind *me* about the parallels between this situation and another we've experienced together. I've just spent the last hour behind bars."

She dragged him to a stop. "I didn't apologize to that photographer, I didn't give him an interview, I didn't pay for his camera, and he still didn't press charges. You can't give in to people like this. They'll just take advantage."

"The photographer from the *Inquisitor* didn't press charges because your grandmother and I paid him very well not to."

She yanked out of his grasp and turned on him, her eyes blazing. "You what?"

"I contacted the photographer and paid him off," Josh replied.

He watched as her temper began to boil uncontrollably. "You . . . creep!" The last word was nearly a shriek. "How could you? Where do you get the idea that you can run my life?"

"Taryn, I—"

She held up her hand, silencing him with her glare. "Don't you even bother with an excuse because I don't want to hear it, buster. Just take me home. Now."

Taryn was ominously silent on the ride home. Josh wasn't sure what he could say to her that he hadn't already said. He was sorry, he regretted his actions and he never meant to hurt her. But she seemed more angry that he'd paid off the photographer from the *Inquisitor*, than that he'd busted L.A.'s most important art critic over the head with a piece of couch art.

Would he ever be able to figure out her mercurial moods? She went from one extreme to another, dragging him right along with her until he felt dazed and battered. Still, he kept coming back for more, as if this hold she had on him could never be broken.

He pulled his car to the curb in front of Taryn's loft, after he'd scanned for photographers. An instant later, Taryn hopped out and headed toward the front door. Josh turned off the ignition, threw the car door open and sprinted after her.

"Taryn! Wait a second."

She turned and held out her hand. "Leave me alone, Josh. I don't feel like talking about this right now. I just want to go to bed and forget this entire day ever happened." She turned back to the door and began to punch in the security code.

Josh stepped up behind her and placed his palm flat on the door to keep her from entering. "What about your paintings? We were going to start tomorrow."

Her shoulders slumped. "Forget it," she said. "It doesn't make any difference. The opening will be a complete flop and a new series of paintings won't help. I might as well just go back to Europe right now."

Josh grabbed her hand and wove his fingers through hers, but she tugged out of his grasp.

"I'm tired," she said, avoiding his gaze. "Please. Let me go."

With that, she turned, pulled the door open, and walked inside without a backward glance. Josh stood outside on the sidewalk for a long time, pacing, trying to decide whether to follow her and force her to discuss her feelings, or whether to leave the discussion for another time.

In the end, he decided to leave. He'd give her the night. But tomorrow, they were going to straighten this whole mess out. And he and Taryn would face the feelings that were raging between them. Tonight, as he had defended Taryn's honor, he had chosen to put his careful, conservative approach behind him. And now, like it or not, Josh Banks had reluctantly become a man of action.

TARYN SLOWLY CLIMBED the three flights of stairs to her loft. She felt utterly exhausted, as if she couldn't take another step. Her mind was numb and her heart ached.

She had wanted so much to believe that she and Josh might have a chance at a relationship. But after tonight, she realized that she'd been deluding herself. At every turn, they seemed to be at odds, on opposite sides of every issue. Her feelings for Josh were so real and so pure, like nothing she'd ever experienced before and she was certain she was feeling the first glimmers of love. But then another catastrophe would erupt between them and all hope would disappear.

No! She couldn't love Josh Banks. He was controlling and stubborn and demanding. She would wither like a flower in the desert under his strict expectations. He'd already ruined her chances for a real life and a career. What more would she have to give up to love him?

She had no choice, she would have to leave. To stay in L.A. would be courting disaster. If she was far enough away, maybe her feelings for him would fade. But where would she go? She couldn't return to Europe. That life was behind her now and she would never, ever go back.

Taryn pushed the key into the lock and pulled the door to her loft open. The room was dark as she walked in and she fumbled for the lights. She tossed her purse on the coffee table, then sank down on the couch. She wasn't sure how long she sat there, her head tipped back, her mind empty. A clatter at the door jerked her upright and she slipped off the couch.

Had Josh decided to press the issue and continue their argument? Taryn pressed her palms against the steel door and hesitantly looked through the peephole.

"Berti!" She unlocked the door and slid it open. "Lord, you scared me! What are you doing here?"

Berti dragged his luggage in. "I came to collect my things," he said.

"What about Margaux? Why did you leave her place?"

"That Margaux, she is a *mégère*. How you say..."

"Shrew?" Taryn offered.

He flopped down on the couch and stretched out. "*Violà. C'est ça!* A shrew. She said I was making her crazy. Well, *she* was making *me* crazy. Crazy as a dead bug."

"Bed bug," Taryn corrected. She pulled his feet off the couch and sat down next to him. "What happened?"

"Well, first, she does not appreciate the fine value and outstanding quality of the Home Shopping Channel."

"What did you buy now?"

"She bought it, *réellement.* I used her credit card. Another pink poodle statue with Austrian crystal eyes. She is French, I thought she would like poodles. My *maman*, she *loves* those little dogs. Who is to know these crazy French women, eh? American women are much more understanding, *non?*"

"Berti , you can't stay here," Taryn said. She drew a deep breath. The time had come to dash his hopes for love and send him home to Maman and Papa Ducharme. It wasn't fair to keep stringing him along as she had. And with Josh out of her life, she couldn't allow herself to fall back into her bad habits.

Berti frowned, ignoring her comment. "You know, I went back to the police station a few days ago."

"You didn't get into more trouble, did you?"

"*Non.* It is not like that. It is something much different."

Taryn covered her ears. "I don't want to hear about another tour, Berti," she said with a sigh. "I'm exhausted. Besides, I have something important to tell you."

"But, *chérie*, this *is* important," he insisted.

Taryn ground her teeth. Lord, the man could be exasperating. "Berti, just listen and don't interrupt."

"Do you remember that lady policeman we met?"

Taryn folded her hands on her lap and plowed ahead. "I know this might hurt you..."

"Julie Knowles is her name. I've invited her to return to Europe with me."

"...and believe me, I really do care about you..."

"Do you know she can disable a man with just the heel of her hand? She is amazing. I have never met anyone like her."

Taryn stopped. "What are you talking about?"

"I have met the woman of my dreams, *chérie,*" Berti crowed.

"Who?"

"Officer Julie Knowles! Of the Beverly Hills Police Department. Badge number 7-6-9."

"That policewoman you met that night I got arrested? But you hardly know her."

"It makes no difference, *chérie.* She has stolen my heart."

She shook her head dubiously. "This is not going to work, Berti. I know you and I know how fickle you are. When you get tired of her, she'll be stranded, all alone in a foreign country. You can't take this woman back to Europe with you."

Berti shook his head. "Oh, *non,* I will not tire of her. If I do, she will break my legs. Or my arms. Or maybe both."

"She told you this?"

"Yes," Berti replied matter-of-factly. "And to tell the truth, I believe her."

Taryn shook her head slowly. "You really think she's right for you?"

"Did you not notice, Tara? She is a big woman. I think she will be just the kind to stand up on *maman*."

"Stand up *to maman*," she corrected, with a smile. "And yes, if anyone could stand up to your *maman*, Officer Knowles could."

"Then you are not angry?" Berti asked.

Taryn smiled, then grabbed his arm and hugged it tight. "No, no, not at all. Maybe you have found the perfect woman for you. Just make sure you treat her right."

Berti shrugged. "I have no choice."

A sigh escaped Taryn's lips. "Good," she murmured, pushing herself up from the couch. "Now, I'm going to bed. I've had a long day and need some sleep."

Berti stood up beside her. "Then we shall say *au revoir* now, *chérie*. Julie and Berti are off to Paris tomorrow. I have a race in three days. Our plane leaves for New York at 2:00 a.m. Julie's friends are going to take us to the airport in a police car."

Taryn threw her arms around Berti's neck and hugged him. "I'll miss you, Berti," Taryn said.

"And I will miss you, Tara," he said. "You will come back to Europe soon, *non?*"

She shrugged. "I don't know. Maybe. Maybe not. But if I come back, I'll be sure to call you and Julie." She smiled, then stood on her tiptoes and kissed him on the cheek. Giving him a little wave, Taryn walked to her room. She closed her bedroom door behind her and crossed to the bed, then flopped down on it, pressing her face into her pillows.

For the first time in many years, she felt completely alone, abandoned. Taryn drew in a deep breath and held it, waiting for the paralyzing fear to grip her. She'd felt the fear every time her parents had walked out the door for another of their extended holidays. She'd felt the terror at the funeral and on the day her grandmother put her on the plane for boarding school. And she'd felt the dread every Christmas when all her school chums would leave for home and she'd be left alone, rattling around the empty hallways of her dormitory.

She swore she'd never let herself feel that way again and to that end, she'd surrounded herself with fawning companions who had nothing better to do with their lives. But now, she had no one. Unless she counted Josh, whom she could have . . . if she wanted him . . . which she didn't. She waited—waited for her breath to catch in her throat and her heart to twist in her chest. Waited for the tears to come. . . .

But nothing came.

Taryn rolled over and brushed her hair out of her eyes. She stared at the ceiling, unaware of her surroundings, only aware that she didn't *feel* anything.

"Maybe I'm not afraid," she murmured. She waited, trying to summon up a knot in her stomach, a wave of nausea. She levered herself up and hugged a pillow to her chest, rocking back and forth impatiently.

Slowly, realization seeped through her mind. "I'm not afraid," she repeated, this time with more conviction. "I'm not." Maybe she could go on, alone, if she had to. She could find a place to live in this world, leaving behind all the doubts and insecurities of her childhood, all the mistakes she'd made in the past. She could try again to build a real life, with her painting. After all, Edwin St. Andrews's influence only reached so far.

Taryn sighed and tipped her head back. But was she really alone? Or was she fooling herself, still hoping, deep inside her heart, that she and Josh might work things out?

7

THE NEWSROOM at the *Los Angeles Post* was a picture of controlled pandemonium as Josh wove through a maze of cubicles in search of Garrett McCabe's desk. The *Post*'s most popular columnist, McCabe worked at home and usually only came into the office to file his installments of "Boys' Night Out." On occasion, he used the bar at Flynn's as his office, writing his column on the backs of bar napkins or on small scraps of paper. Josh had even seen him compose a column in his head, then recite every word he'd "written" before he rushed off to make his deadline.

He'd checked both McCabe's apartment and the bar at Flynn's looking for his friend, before he headed downtown to the newspaper's offices. The receptionist informed him that Garrett was indeed in, and after a lengthy search, Josh found a cubicle with his friend's name on it. It was empty.

Stepping inside, Josh searched for a place to sit down and wait, but both chairs were stacked with magazines, file folders, and newspapers. He picked up a magazine from the top of a pile and flipped through it distractedly, then realized that he was paging through a lingerie catalog.

Josh glanced around to make sure no one was watching before he adjusted his glasses and closely scrutinized the small scraps of lace and silk. The appeal was undeniable. His gaze was caught by pair of black bikinis like the pair Taryn had worn on Zuma Beach, and his mind wandered back to the feel of her skin against his palms, her slender body as she danced around him in the sand.

She'd been so wild and free, all bright light and passionate color. And then he'd reprimanded her, and she seemed to fade before his eyes. Suddenly his obligation to Olivia seemed more like a burden. If it wasn't for his promise, he could have allowed her to tear the rest of her clothes off and play in the surf. He could have joined her if he had wanted.

A wrenching realization hit him like a slap across the face. What if Olivia wasn't nominated? He'd have no excuse to see Taryn again. The reasons that brought them together would suddenly become irrelevant and Taryn could go on with her life as she pleased. Josh would have no reason to stop her.

"You looking for McCabe?"

Josh glanced up. A skinny young man leaned up against the opening to Garrett's work space. He couldn't be much older than nineteen or twenty, but his short-cropped hair and smooth face made him look even younger. He stared down at the lingerie catalog, his eyes wide. Josh hastily tossed the catalog back on top of the pile, then rubbed his palms together. "Ah, yes," Josh replied. "I'm a—a friend of his."

The kid held out his hand. "Alex Armstrong, sports," he said, schooling his squeaky voice into an authoritarian tone.

Josh took his hand and shook it. "Josh Banks," he said. "Accountant."

"My name really isn't Alex," he explained. "It's Alvin. But Alex sounds better, don't you think? More macho. I'm conducting sort of an informal poll on the name thing. I think it's probably the most important decision a reporter has to make, don't you think?"

"I don't know," Josh replied.

"I mean, it's tough enough to make it in the rough-and-tumble world of sports, so I've got to watch every move I make, from the choice of my clothing to the tone of my voice. I've been working on the voice. Strong, authoritative, in charge. Don't you think?"

"I—I guess," Josh replied.

"Armstrong, are you bothering my buddy Josh?" Garrett stepped up behind the skinny Alvin, placed his hands on the boy's shoulders and steered him out of the cubicle. "Rowdy's looking for you. He needs a copy of the Lakers' schedule from last year. And if he sends you out for sandwiches, like the slave driver he is, can you pick me up a ham on rye?"

"Ham on rye. Mustard, but no mayo, right? Got it, Mr. McCabe." Alvin held out his hand again and once again, Josh shook it. "Pleasure meeting you, Mr. Banks," he said. "And thanks for the advice. I really, really appreciate it."

As he turned to rush off, Alvin ran smack into the wall of Garrett's cubicle. Like a pinball, he just bounced off. "Sorry," he murmured, a beet red flush creeping up his neck.

Garrett chuckled while the kid struggled to compose himself and make a proper exit. "Interns," he muttered. "The pestilence of the newspaper business. Don't get me wrong, he's a nice kid and he knows every baseball statistic ever recorded. But he's so damn enthusiastic, it's exhausting. Makes me feel old. Was I ever that enthusiastic?"

"Probably," Josh said.

Garrett cleared his guest chair with one swipe of his hand and did the same for his own chair before sitting down. "So, this is a surprise. What brings you down here?" he asked, propping his feet on the edge of his desk.

A sudden fear gripped McCabe's expression. "Our apartment building didn't burn down, did it?"

Josh frowned. "I don't think so," he replied.

He sat back and relaxed, then bounced forward again. "Aw, geez, I've been burglarized, haven't I? I was going to ask Amberson to replace that damn lock, but I just never got around to it."

Josh shook his head. "Actually, I came to ask a favor."

Garrett cocked his head with curiosity. "You're asking *me* for a favor? Hey, you got it, buddy."

"I need you to introduce me to Edwin St. Andrews," Josh said.

"Why would you want an introduction to that old gasbag?" Garrett asked.

"We have an important . . . matter to discuss."

Garrett watched him, an inquisitive arch to his brow. "What's this all about?"

"It's a private matter," Josh said.

"Ahh." Garrett nodded. "Taryn Wilde, right?"

"I guess you didn't see last night's episode of 'Art Exposed.'"

"'Art Exposed?' I didn't see it, but I've heard about it. Edwin's been ranting about that show all morning. Some guy busted him over the head with a—" Garrett frowned. "You're the hooligan who attacked our resident gasbag?"

Josh nodded dejectedly. "I don't know what came over me. I must have been insane. The guy made me so damn angry." In fact, Josh had never acted out of anger in his life. Or made such a huge error in judgment. But after the last twenty-four hours, he wasn't sure just who he really was anymore—or who he was becoming. Josh Banks, hotheaded tough guy, didn't quite sit right with him.

"A lot of guys around here are going to want to meet you," Garrett said. "In just one morning, you've become legendary at the *L.A. Post.* Like another Woodward or Bernstein."

"I may be a legend, but I've got some major damage control to take care of."

If he could only fix his mistake, maybe Taryn could still have a successful gallery showing. St. Andrews was the key and Josh was willing to do just about anything to get the critic to give Taryn a stay of execution. If he succeeded, she would paint her masterpiece, and she would stay in L.A. And if he was lucky, she'd give him another chance.

If, if, if. His entire future hinged on a series of optimistic outcomes. And the biggest if of all? If Olivia won the nomination, he'd still have a reason to spend time with Taryn.

Garrett slid his feet to the floor, then leaned forward in his chair, his elbows braced on his knees. "In that case, I'm not sure I'm the one to make the introductions, Josh. Last month I took the little guillotine Edwin keeps on his desk and used it to chop the heads off of a canful of sardines. The month before, I coated his pencils with hemorrhoid cream. And before that, I changed all the memory dials on his office phone to 1-900-HOT-LIPS."

"Maybe you could just show me where his desk is?" Josh suggested.

"No problem," Garrett said. "He's two rows over and three cubes up. Look for the poster of Mona Lisa with the Groucho Marx mustache and eyebrows. My latest contribution to art appreciation."

Josh smiled. "Thanks, McCabe."

"No problem. Just yell if you need backup. And don't take any of his crap. It's all a big act. Ten years ago, Edwin was selling shoes on Rodeo Drive."

"I appreciate the advice," Josh said.

"Good luck, buddy. And I hope Taryn Wilde is worth it."

"She is," Josh said. He followed Garrett's directions, but with every step he took toward a confrontation with Edwin, he wondered whether he was going to make the situation worse.

How much worse could it possibly get? Taryn was talking about leaving Los Angeles, giving up on her gallery showing. In *his* mind, there wasn't anything worse than the prospect of losing her. A mustachioed Mona Lisa beckoned with a coy smile and Josh stepped up to the art critic's cubicle.

"Mr. St. Andrews?"

His back to Josh, the critic continued to work at his computer terminal, refusing to be bothered with an interruption.

"Mr. St. Andrews, I'd like to talk to you."

The man typed for a moment longer, then sighed disgustedly, still refusing to turn around. "It doesn't take a higher form of intelligence to see that I'm busy. In my infinite wisdom, I've already deduced that you're merely a dullard who's mistaken me for someone who might be willing to converse with you. Go away, now. Before I'm forced to raise my voice and thoroughly humiliate you."

"I don't think you'll want to do that," Josh replied.

The critic spun around in his chair, his face mottled with anger. But as soon as he caught sight of Josh, his complexion paled visibly. He scrambled out of his chair and backed away from Josh, surprisingly nimble and quick for such a large man.

"Stay away from me," he warned. "We settled our business at the police station." His lower lip quivered slightly and his hands shook. Could Edwin the Executioner actually be frightened of him? Josh Banks, hotheaded tough guy, decided to test the theory and took a step forward.

"I'll call security," Edwin cried. "You won't get away with this. I—I'm a very important member of the staff here."

"I don't want to hurt you, Mr. St. Andrews. . . ." He left the statement hanging and allowed Edwin to attach whatever finish he cared to. The simple fact was, he *didn't* want to hurt the guy. But there was no sense letting him know that.

"What *do* you want?" Edwin demanded.

"I'd like to talk to you about Taryn Wilde."

"What about her?"

"I think you treated her unfairly last night."

"So?" Edwin said, regaining a small measure of his haughty attitude. "I treat plenty of artists unfairly. That's my job." He sniffed, then straightened his tie.

"Well, in this case, I think you better make it your job to figure out a way to repair the damage you've done."

"The damage I've done?" he huffed.

"I'm concerned about Taryn, and when I'm concerned, I do something about it. If you get my meaning." He knew there was a reason he'd felt compelled to see *The Godfather* seven times. A wise guy attitude went a long way in enhancing his persuasive skills.

Edwin swallowed, his Adam's apple bobbing nervously. "As I asked before, what do you want?"

"I was thinking of a trade. You take care of Taryn, and I'll take care of you."

"How can you take care of me?"

"Taxes," Josh said.

"You—You're with the IRS?" Edwin gasped. This time all the color drained out of his face.

"Not exactly. But I have contacts there," Josh lied. "I understand you filed a very... creative return last year." Edwin's knees buckled slightly and Josh stifled a satisfied smile. When it came to taxes, he had to admit, he had great instincts. He could smell a cheat a mile away. And by the look in Edwin St. Andrews's eyes, the guy had more than a few questionable deductions floating around in his tax history.

"It would be a real shame if you had to go through an audit. All that time and those penalties. And they can go back years."

Edwin gulped. "Years?"

Josh nodded solemnly. "You'll need a good tax accountant." He let him sweat a little longer before he reached into his breast pocket, pulled out his business card and handed it to Edwin. "It just so happens, I am a tax accountant. The best in Beverly Hills. And I'm willing to offer my services in return for your cooperation."

"What if they don't audit me?" Edwin asked stubbornly.

"Sooner or later, they'll get you," Josh said. "But I like to take a preventative approach to taxes. My clients get audited, they come out without a scratch."

The man studied him for a long moment. "Let's say we make a deal. I can't write a good review," he explained. "I *never* write a good review. My readers wouldn't know what to think if I did. A mediocre review is all I can offer."

"I'm not asking for false praise, Edwin, just a fair shot. If she's good, I want you to say so."

"I've seen her work at the Talbot Gallery. She's good. She has a rather intense, though somewhat unfocused, passion. I can promise you that a mediocre review from me will assure Ms. Wilde a resounding success."

"You're not trying to hustle me, are you, Edwin? Because I don't like to be hustled."

"No. I swear. I'm not trying to . . ." He sniffed again, as if the word were too repugnant to utter. "Hustle you."

"All right," Josh conceded. "We have a deal. And Edwin?"

"Yes?"

"Don't make me regret this." With that, Josh turned and walked back along the route he came. He'd accomplished what he'd come for. Media relations were now back on track. Taryn's reputation as an artist was unsullied.

As Josh walked by Garrett's cubicle to thank him, he found his friend sprawled in his chair, a computer printout stretched in front of him. He looked up and grinned at Josh, then held out the paper. "The Academy Award nominations just came in over the wire. Olivia's on the list."

Josh smiled, a wave of relief washing over him. "Then I'd say this day has definitely taken a turn for the better. I'd better stop over at Olivia's. She's going to want to discuss the budget for publicity and her award night wardrobe. And she'll probably want to throw a party."

And after he met with Olivia, it was time to finally settle things once and for all with Taryn Wilde.

TARYN SAT ON the hardwood floor of her loft, her knees tucked under her chin, her loose cotton skirt twisted around her legs. An abstract self-portrait, propped against the wall, stared back at her. Though she remembered the time, three years ago, when she had painted the portrait, she couldn't recall the woman in the painting. It was as if she looked at a stranger, rendered in brilliant blobs and swashes of oil paint.

The painting was good, though not her most mature work. But in every stroke of the brush she saw passion, and emotion in each choice of color. She'd tried to recapture that feeling over and over again during her time in Los Angeles, but had only been able to produce a few unfinished canvases.

Margaux had been thrilled with that halfhearted work, claiming the paintings represented a new level of sensitivity. Taryn tried to believe her and pushed forward with her work, but there was something missing inside. How ironic that once she'd set her sights on a career as a painter her artistic muse had decided it was time for a long holiday and hadn't bothered to leave a forwarding address.

Taryn groaned and buried her face in her hands. Why even try? Josh had ruined any chance of a successful showing. Edwin St. Andrews would vilify her in the press. An image of "The Executioner" flashed in her mind, torn canvas and a stretcher hanging around his neck like some bizarre piece of jewelry. She groaned again and her thoughts drifted to Josh's expression at that moment, as his anger transformed to a mixture of surprise and regret. Maybe she should have been pleased that he'd defended her so nobly. But an overly protective attitude certainly didn't justify his impulsive actions.

A shrill buzz echoed through the loft, startling Taryn out of her contemplation. She glanced over at the security intercom, her brow furrowed. She wasn't expecting company—Berti had jetted off to Paris early that morning with his new love, Officer Knowles, and Margaux was in Santa Barbara for the day. She had no other friends. No doubt, the tabloid reporters were back, spurred on by her ignominious appearance on "Art Exposed."

She scrambled to her feet and ran to the door, then punched at the intercom button. "Go away!" she shouted. "Just leave me alone! I have no comment!"

"Taryn?" Josh's voice crackled through the speaker. "Taryn, let me in."

She closed her eyes and leaned back against the wall. No, she wouldn't let him in. What good would seeing Josh do for either one of them? Apart, they were safe from public humiliation. But together, who could predict what new disaster was waiting around the next corner?

She turned back to the intercom. "I said, go way and leave me alone."

"Taryn, I have to talk to you. I'm coming up."

"Where do you get off thinking you can just order me around?" she demanded.

"I'm not ordering you, I'm merely informing you of fact. I'm coming up and we *are* going to talk."

"You can't get through the security door if I don't buzz you up," Taryn countered. "Besides, I have nothing more to say to say to you." She paused, but he didn't reply. "You're just going to have to stop bossing me around. I think it would be best if you stay as far away from me as possible. Lately, the only time I seem to get into any trouble is when I'm with you. And then I'm always to blame. So, if you're really serious about protecting Olivia's reputation, do it from a safe distance. I won't be responsible for—"

Her words were interrupted by a barrage of pounding on her front door. Her gaze darted between the door and the intercom. She pushed the button again. "Josh?" Silence. "Josh, are you still there?" When there was still no answer, Taryn stepped to the door and looked through the peephole. The pounding had stopped and Josh stood outside, calmly waiting for her to open the door. Meanwhile, she'd been talking to an empty lobby.

Taryn's temper ignited. Of all the overbearing, insolent—was there no end to his bullying? He never listened to anything she said, he just ignored her and continued on his own course. He'd probably kicked the lobby door open. What had happened to the shy, unassuming man she'd met a month ago? She flipped the lock and yanked the door open.

"I told you to go away!" she shouted.

He pushed past her into the loft. "I'm not leaving until we talk."

She turned on him, her arms akimbo. "This is just like you! Pushy. Dictatorial. Arrogant. Well, I'm tired of you interfering in my life. From the moment you first walked in that door, you've done nothing but cause me grief. You want me to promise to behave? Fine. Anything to get you out of my hair for good."

"Is that what you really want, Taryn?"

No, it wasn't what she wanted, but there wasn't a chance in a million she'd let him know how she really felt about him. He didn't care about her. All he really cared about was Olivia and her damn award. If she said it enough, she'd convince herself. "Yes," she said, trying to make her words sound resolute. "That's what I want."

"What about your painting? What about the new series?"

"There isn't going to be a new series. If Margaux can't do with what she has already, she can hire a monkey to paint a new series. It doesn't make a difference anyway. The show is guaranteed to be a total bust."

"It's not like you to give up so easily," Josh said.

"What do you know about me?" she countered. "In all of this mess, have you even bothered to consider what's important to me?" She shook her head and held out her hand to stop his reply. "If you had, you would never have attacked Edwin St. Andrews. All you cared about was your proper little agenda, Olivia's precious award. You don't know anything about me."

"I know you're a painter," Josh said. "A damn good painter...with a rather intense, but unfocused, passion." Edwin's words came back to him and he smiled inwardly. It sounded like a rather erudite commentary even to his unartistic ears.

Taryn scoffed. "What are you talking about?"

"I—I'm not sure," he said, frowning. "I guess I'm saying that a painter paints. Yeah, that's it. A painter doesn't sit around pouting like some—some spoiled brat."

"I'm not a spoiled brat," Taryn replied petulantly. "And maybe I don't feel like painting right now, Warden."

Josh pulled off his suit jacket and neatly folded it before he draped it across the back of the couch. "That's too bad," he replied. Slowly, he unknotted his tie, then removed his cuff links. "Because I kind of feel like posing right now."

"What?" Taryn blinked in disbelief.

"Well, I was hoping that when you stopped feeling sorry for yourself, you might want to get back to work. And I'm here to help."

"You're going to pose for me?"

"We've discussed this all before, haven't we?" Josh asked.

Taryn laughed. "Isn't this just great! Now's a fine time for you to decide to get naked. After you've ruined any chance I might have for a decent showing. I don't need those paintings now."

Josh unbuttoned the top button of his crisply starched shirt. "Where do you want me?" he asked.

She watched him suspiciously, her eyes drawn to his fingers as he worked another button open. "Don't toy with me, Josh Banks. I don't know what sick little game you and Olivia have cooked up now, but I *do* know that you have no intention of taking your clothes off in front of me. You might as well leave right now before you embarrass yourself."

"Don't believe me?" Josh asked. He slid his tie out from around his collar then held it out to her. When she didn't reach for it, he let it drop to the floor.

"This isn't going to work," Taryn said. "I don't want you to pose for me." Temptation flooded her senses and she fought back a wave of desire. If Josh Banks removed his clothes, she'd be in big trouble. How could she sit calmly sketching him, when she really wanted to drag him into the bedroom and find the passion she'd been missing for so long?

He unbuttoned a third button, exposing a glimpse of hair on his chest. "Come on, Taryn. Are you going to let a guy like Edwin St. Andrews run your life?" he asked.

"Why would I let Edwin run my life when *you're* doing such a good job?" she replied acerbically.

"Now you're making more sense." He tugged his shirttails out of his trousers. "Where do you want me?" He quickly unbuttoned the rest of his shirt then pulled it off. As Taryn's gaze dropped to his chest, her breath stopped in her throat. The man was not meant to wear a business suit. He wasn't meant to wear anything at all.

His chest was broad and smooth with a silky dusting of hair that followed an intriguing path from his collarbone to his flat belly, before disappearing beneath the waist of his pleated trousers. His skin gleamed a honey brown and Taryn wondered how that could be for a man who wore a suit from dawn to dusk.

Her fingers clenched and she fought an overwhelming urge to touch him, the same way she wanted to touch a Michelangelo or a Rodin, with reverence and awe. But he was no cold, carved piece of marble; he was a warm, breathing, flesh-and-bone man. Her pulse quickened as she imagined the feel of his skin beneath her lips, the taste and smell of him. His hands moved to his belt buckle and she swallowed hard.

"I—I'm not really ready for you right now."

Josh dropped his hands to his sides and smiled. "Maybe you should get ready," he suggested, "before I go any further. I wouldn't want to catch cold."

"Yes," Taryn said. "I should." She stood rooted in her spot, suddenly unable to remember what it was she was supposed to do next, and just as suddenly forgetting her prior resolve. Something—or someone—had scrambled her senses like eggs in an omelet factory.

"Don't you have to make some sketches first?" Josh prompted.

"Yes. Yes, that's right. Sketches. I'll go get my pad and charcoal." She dragged a stool from the kitchen counter and placed it beneath the skylight. "Sit down here," she said. She rushed toward her bedroom, then stopped and turned back to him. "And don't take any more of your clothes off."

As soon as Taryn reached the safe confines of her room, she closed the door behind her. She drew in a deep breath and then placed her palms on her cheeks. What was happening to her? She felt warm, flushed from head to toe and all she'd seen of his body so far was his chest.

"He's just a mass of muscle and bone," Taryn muttered to herself. "You're an artist and he's a model. And you've done this hundreds of times before." But it was hard to think of Josh as Everyman, a man without a finite identity. Like it or not, she was falling in love with him.

It's just that she'd imagined the first time he took his clothes off in her presence there would be something more interesting in store for them than painting. But Josh Banks had come here with noble intentions. He had come to help her with her painting, not to seduce her. At least that's what he wanted her to believe.

Gathering her composure, Taryn walked out of the bedroom, a smile fixed on her face. Josh had given her an opportunity. And she wasn't about to blow it due to some disobedient hormones. She would paint Josh Banks or swoon trying. And her show would be an unqualified success, with or without Edwin St. Andrews's blessing. She'd deal with her ridiculous infatuation later.

He was still sitting on the stool when she returned, but he'd removed his glasses. For an instant, she became lost in his dark eyes, then, with a silent reprimand, she forced herself to pull her gaze away. "I—I must have left my sketch pad out here," she explained. She walked over to her worktable and found it right where she'd dropped it, amidst her palettes and paints and brushes.

"Do you want me to take my pants off now?" Josh asked. She spun around and stared at him. Odd that he didn't seem to be the least hesitant about the offer. At one time, he would have hemmed and hawed at the prospect. But now, it was as if he were testing her, pushing her to the far edges of her resolve. Was this really all about posing for her or did he have another hidden agenda? If he did, at least she knew Olivia wasn't behind this one.

"No, that's not necessary. Not right now. I'd like you to turn slightly to the side and bring your leg up on the rung of the stool." He obediently did as he was told. "I want to see both your back and your profile." He adjusted. "Tip your face up to the light." He adjusted again. "No, that's not right. Lower."

After she'd given him four or five more directions, she realized that it would be impossible to position him without touching him. Steeling her determination, she stepped forward and grasped his shoulders, tilting the left slightly lower. When she was satisfied, she pulled her hands away, watching as they trembled slightly. She hurried to grab another stool from the kitchen, then perched atop it, ready to sketch.

With a steadfast show of concentration, she worked, all the while aware of a strange tension that hung in the air. He didn't speak, didn't move, but she could see him breathing in the subtle shift of sinew across his back. She completed three detailed sketches of his torso, all of them very promising, but finished only from the waist up. If she planned to go on, she'd have to ask him to remove his trousers.

She swallowed hard, then cleared her throat. "I think it's time to—to—"

"Take off my pants?" Josh asked.

"Yes," she replied in a choked voice. "If you have no . . . objections."

"None at all," Josh said.

With his back to her, he removed his shoes and socks, then unbuckled his belt and unzipped his pants. The sound of the zipper reverberated through the loft, so loud she felt like covering her ears. His trousers dropped to the floor and he reached for the waist of his silk boxers.

"That's enough," she cried. "For now."

He looked over his shoulder. "Are you sure?"

"Positive," she replied. "Find your place so I can begin again."

Fifteen minutes later, her sketches were complete, except for the part of him covered by his silk boxers. She'd seen enough backsides to improvise and she imagined his would be one of the best. Her thoughts wandered in other directions—to the rest of his anatomy hidden beneath the boxers. Vivid images careered through her mind. He would be perfect—everywhere.

Taryn closed her eyes and gave herself another mental tongue-lashing. This fantasizing would have to stop. When she opened her eyes, her gaze came to rest on his legs. They were long and nicely shaped. "You have very well-formed gastrocnemius muscles," she commented. He turned around to face her, his expression questioning. "Ca—calf muscles," she explained.

"I run," he replied. "On the beach."

"I had to study anatomy as part of my figure drawing course at the Sorbonne," she babbled. "I know all the important muscle groups." Idle conversation about anatomy seemed to put both of them at ease, diminishing the unbearable tension that had grown between them and taking her mind off his body.

"This is all very interesting," Josh replied. "Do you want me to take off my shorts now?"

Startled by his offhand question, she fought the impulse to say yes. She felt a sudden urge to substantiate her assessment of the man beneath the boxers. So much for idle conversation. "No!" she cried. "I mean, you don't have to. Not yet. Why don't I try some sketches from this angle?"

He faced her now, watching her every move, his gaze probing hers. She sketched frantically, only looking up at him when she absolutely had to. "Tip your head up slightly." She watched as he closed his eyes and angled his chin up to the skylight. As the early afternoon light spilled over his face, a tiny moan escaped her lips at the sheer masculine beauty she saw. Josh Banks was likely the most handsome man she'd ever met. Why hadn't she noticed that before?

As if drawn into a trance, she walked up to him and placed her hand under his chin, positioning him until the planes of his cheeks glinted with softly diffused sunlight. He opened his eyes and her gaze was trapped by his. She spread her fingers against his jaw. Slowly, he raised his hand and captured hers, then placed a kiss in the center of her palm.

She held her breath, every nerve of her body focused on the pressure of his mouth on her skin. This shouldn't be happening, her mind screamed. But she wanted him to continue. He looked directly into her eyes, their gazes level as he sat on the stool. As he waited for her approval, she saw his expression flood with desire. She drew a shaky breath and he pulled her between his legs, his heels braced on the bottom rung of the stool, his hands encircling her waist.

The pad and charcoal dropped to the floor, the sketch now forgotten. She didn't care about her paintings or her gallery showing or anything beyond this man's embrace. Slowly, she skimmed her palms up his arms to his shoulders. His muscles bunched and flexed beneath her hands as he touched the top button on her sleeveless blouse.

"We shouldn't do this," Taryn murmured, not believing her words for a single second.

He undid the top two buttons and slid his hands inside the neck of her blouse. "I know," he replied, the corners of his mouth curving up. "It's reckless and impulsive."

She kissed his smile. "Exactly the kind of behavior you're always warning me against," she added.

"I'll admit, I may have been wrong...about a few things," Josh said.

Taryn wrapped her arms around his neck. "I'm glad you've finally seen the error of your ways."

Josh touched his lips to hers, a gentle, fleeting caress, filled with provocative possibilities. "I'm counting on you to misbehave," he breathed. "Starting right now."

With that, he wove his fingers through her hair and brought her mouth down to his. His tongue teased at her lips, tasting and tantalizing until she moaned in frustration and opened her mouth to him. Their tongues touched hesitantly, and then more aggressively, until the kiss deepened, becoming almost frantic in its need.

His taste seeped into her blood, warm and liquid, like a narcotic, both soothing and pleasantly addictive. She'd been so long without a man, yet in all her experience, she'd never remembered feeling such powerful desire over a simple kiss.

For the first time in her life, she realized that a kiss could be more than just a physical meeting of mouths. And this kiss was confirmation of everything she'd always dreamed of. Here was a man she could love, honorable and honest, a man who wasn't afraid to challenge her and to make her the best person she could be.

Taryn drew back and watched his shuttered gaze as she slowly unbuttoned her blouse. He impatiently pushed her hands away and finished the job for her, then nudged the garment off her shoulders. A long sigh slipped from his throat. He closed his eyes and explored her exposed skin with his fingertips.

"You're so beautiful," he murmured. "I've imagined touching you like this, but I never thought it would feel so—" he pulled in a deep breath through clenched teeth, and let it out slowly "—good," he finished, his eyes closed.

She reached for the clasp on the front of her bra and unhooked it, shrugging her shoulders until the straps slid down along her shoulders and the black lace fluttered to the floor behind her. Gently, she drew his hands to her breasts. He opened his eyes lazily and his hungry gaze drifted downward.

He studied her for a long time, his hands still, his breathing labored. She reached over and brushed a lock of hair from his forehead, then smoothed his pensive expression away with her fingers. As if startled from a dream, he glanced up at her and smiled hesitantly. As their gazes locked again, she reached behind her and unfastened her skirt. It slithered over her hips and down her legs, then puddled on the floor around her bare feet.

Placing his feet on the floor between hers, Josh drew her thigh up against his hip. He reached for her other thigh and suddenly she found herself on his lap, her legs wrapped around his waist. They balanced precariously on the stool and she was afraid to move, afraid he'd let go. She had no choice but to hang on.

She'd fought him for so long, fought his need to control her. And now she wanted to relinquish it all, to watch him discover the passion that lay hidden inside her, the way a sculptor finds a masterpiece beneath layers of granite.

Take me, her mind sang out. *Take me and make me yours.*

Taryn arched her back and locked her ankles behind him until the hard ridge of his erection pressed against her softness. Through the two layers of silk, his shorts and her panties, she could feel every inch of him and she knew that she had been right. He was perfect in every way.

Josh traced a line of kisses from the base of her throat to the tip of one breast, before teasing at the hardened bud with his lips. Shifting against his lap, she pressed herself closer, willing him to take her taut nipple into his mouth, needing the drenching sensations to continue. She felt a knot of tension begin to grow at her core.

"Taryn, stop," he growled, his breath warm against her breast.

"Stop what?" she murmured, her voice husky with desire.

"Stop wiggling or this is going to be over before we even get started."

Taryn grabbed a fistful of his hair and gently tugged his head up. She smiled mischievously. "Then stop teasing and get started," she said. "I don't want to wait any longer, Josh. We've waited too long already." She kissed his mouth, hard and demanding, until he groaned in response. Cupping her backside in his hands, he stood up and carried her toward the bedroom, her legs still wrapped around his waist.

Taryn waited for the doubts and fears to assail her now, for the trepidation to set in. When it didn't come, she knew why. In the past, impulse and uninhibited lust had always been an adequate substitute for emotional commitment, and physical pleasure and release, for romance and love. Sex had always felt incomplete. But now, for the first time in her life, she had a chance to have it all.

Josh gently lowered her to the bed. She opened her eyes and found him standing over her, watching as she luxuriated in the soft, goose down duvet. "Come here," she said, holding out her arms.

"Not yet," he murmured. "I'll be right back." He padded out of the bedroom and returned moments later with a small foil packet in his hand.

Taryn smiled. "So practical," she teased. "Tell me, are you ever unprepared?"

"Only once," Josh replied, staring down at her. "I was unprepared for you. I never knew I could feel this way. I can't control you, Taryn. I never really could, even though I tried like hell. And now, that's the last thing I want to do."

"Good," Taryn said. "I was starting to get a little tired of fighting you. Now, I think it's about time you took off those shorts, don't you?"

Josh smiled and she thought she saw a faint blush steal up his cheeks. He hooked his thumbs in the waistband of his silk boxer shorts and pushed them down over his hips. She did the same with her bikinis, her eyes still fixed on his body.

Taryn had sketched a lot of naked men over the past ten years, but as she looked at Josh's body, she had absolutely no desire to pick up a sketch pad and pencil. Instead, she wanted to touch him, to feel his passion beneath her fingers. As he lowered himself to the bed, she took his rigid desire in her hand, stroking him until he moaned in response.

Gently, she took the package from his hand and tore it open, then sheathed him. In the next instant, he was above her, his hardness probing at her moist entrance. And then he was deep inside, their bodies so close, joined so intimately.

They may experience it again and again, the soft moans of passion, the sweet lovemaking, the shattering climaxes and the hazy aftermath. But Taryn knew this first time would always be special. Because it was the first time her heart and soul was filled with love for the man that moved above her. She loved Josh Banks with her entire being.

Later, as darkness stole over the bedroom, Taryn slipped from Josh's embrace. He lay sprawled across the bed, the sheets tangled beneath him, his limbs loose with sleep and his beautiful face almost boyish. Taryn grabbed a T-shirt from the bedpost and pulled it on, then padded out of the bedroom to retrieve her sketch pad and charcoal.

She sketched him in the dim light from a bedside lamp until she couldn't keep her eyes open any longer and the charcoal kept slipping from her fingers. Then she flipped off the light and crawled back into bed with him, curling up against his warm body. Stirring, he turned and gathered her in his arms, his mouth seeking hers.

They made love again, and when Taryn finally fell asleep in the early morning hours, she wondered if she could ever fall sleep without him again.

JOSH SLOWLY OPENED his eyes to the morning light. For an instant, he wasn't sure where he was. But then, as he drew a slow breath, he remembered. The sweet scent of Taryn and their lovemaking teased at his nose. She lay next to him, curled beneath the sheets, while he lay on top. He grabbed the edge of the sheet and pulled it up over him, then drew her body against his for warmth.

When he had settled her in the curve of his body, he nuzzled her neck. "Are you awake?"

"Umm," she moaned. "What time is it?"

"It's late," he whispered, placing a kiss on her bare shoulder.

"Do you have to go to work?"

"No, not yet. I'm the boss. I can come in late if I want."

She snuggled closer. "Go back to sleep, then."

"Taryn, I need you to do something for me."

She growled softly and pressed her backside into the curve of his lap. "You're insatiable," she whispered, wriggling against him playfully.

He chuckled and kissed the soft spot at the base of her neck. "That's not what I want. At least, not right this minute." He drew a deep breath, then let it out slowly. "Olivia is throwing a small party tonight. She got a nomination for Best-Supporting Actress. I'd like you to come with me."

Taryn turned in his arms and faced him, her sleepy eyes regarding him suspiciously. He brushed a lock of hair from her forehead and twisted it around his finger. "Josh, I don't think you understand how it is between Olivia and me."

"I know exactly how it is," he replied. "But you're going to be part of my life now, and she's very important to me, too. You're family, Taryn, and it's time for both of you to recognize that fact."

Taryn stiffened in his arms. "We're related, but we're not family. I never had a family, even when my parents were alive."

Josh placed his forehead against hers. "Sweetheart, it's time for a truce."

Taryn sighed and pushed against his shoulders. "A truce," she repeated. "See, this is just like you, Josh. Just because you want something, doesn't make it so. You can't tell me what to do at every turn. This is a big problem between us and I think—"

"*I* think it's important to our future," Josh interrupted. Josh liked the sound of the word, the concept of a future, of a happily-ever-after with Taryn. But by the stubborn look on her face, Taryn had her own opinions about the matter.

"Our future?" she asked. "What future? Who said we had a future, Josh? We spent the night together and suddenly you're mapping out my life for me!"

He smiled and placed his finger over her lips to silence her. "We started something last night, Taryn, and I don't want anything to come between us—especially Olivia."

Taryn frowned. "Maybe last night was just a . . . a one-night stand. Did you ever consider that?"

"No," Josh replied firmly. "And I'd prefer you'd not think of it in that way. I don't sleep with just anyone." He stared at her meaningfully, waiting for her to respond in kind.

"What?" she asked defensively. "You think I do?"

"I didn't say that," Josh replied.

Taryn paused as if she weren't quite sure how to proceed. "All right," she acquiesced. "Let's just say maybe we do have a future, hypothetically speaking. If we did, then you'd have to understand that you can't *make* me do this."

"I wouldn't ask unless it was very important," he murmured, punctuating his request with a soft kiss.

Taryn watched him through sooty lashes. "This is not fair, using sex as a weapon. We're going to have to discuss this." He kissed her again, this time more deeply. She moaned. "All right, all right, I'll go," she said. "But I'm going alone. That way, when this whole thing blows up in your face, I'll be able to leave."

"It won't blow up. We're going to make this work, Taryn. I promise you."

"Just because you say it's going to work, doesn't make it so," she said, echoing her earlier words.

"It will work," Josh said. "So, it's your turn, now. What do you want? Ask me for anything and I'll do it."

Taryn pushed the sheets back and crawled on top of him, straddling his hips. "I don't know if you have what it takes to give me what I want right now," she murmured.

He pushed his hips up and pressed his erection into the soft folds of flesh between her legs. "Sweetheart, I'm going to do my best to give you everything you want, from this moment on."

8

TARYN STOOD on the quiet Westwood street and tugged on the brim of her slouchy straw hat to shade her eyes against the late afternoon sun. Her grandmother's modest home seemed to stare back at her disapprovingly, as if sensing she were an unwelcome guest. An overwhelming sense of dread kept her feet fixed to the concrete, hindering all her attempts to drag herself back into her car, yet impeding her progress to the front door. She'd actually gotten lost trying to find the house that had, for a short time, been her home. Surely that had been an omen. She should have just kept on driving.

How could she possibly face her grandmother now, after so many years of distance and hostility between them? Though she hadn't seen Olivia in over ten years, she still remembered the angry words that they'd parted with—the blame, the recriminations, the insults. But they were the words of a stubborn and capricious teenager, a girl who had yet to come to terms with the dismal hand she'd been dealt in life.

As that girl had grown older, she'd come to realize that Olivia Wilde wasn't entirely to blame for what for her life was, and had become. All Taryn had really wanted from Olivia was the approval her parents had so steadfastly withheld. She hadn't understood that Olivia, too, was ill-prepared to be a parent. So she rebelled, hoping to hurt her grandmother as much as she herself hurt inside. And after that first small rebellion and the attention it gained, it became a way of life, a way to soothe the pain of her childhood, a feeble attempt to force Olivia to love her.

Josh was right. It was time to put the past behind her and begin a new life. She was a different person now. And Olivia was the only family she had left. Though she knew they'd never be close, at least they could acknowledge and respect the fact they were related. It was a small favor Josh had asked from her, one she felt prepared to grant.

Though she'd tried to convince herself that her relationship with Josh could remain purely physical, she sensed he wanted more—and so did she. Josh was not the type to enjoy a casual fling. And deep inside, she knew she had never really felt good about the shallow aspects of her former relationships. Josh was a man she could love, maybe even *did* love. And though they still had a whole lot of negotiating to do, she'd decided to give a little on the subject of her grandmother. For him.

Taryn disengaged her feet from the pavement, walked up to the front door and rang the bell. As it swung open, she drew a deep breath and pasted a smile on her face. But her grandmother did not appear from behind the ornately carved door. Instead, a uniformed maid returned her smile and stepped aside, inviting her to enter. She'd been granted a brief reprieve. Maybe it was another omen.

The large living area was filled with guests, all of them talking and laughing and drinking champagne. From the safety of the foyer, she covertly searched the room for Olivia and found her standing near the fireplace. Josh stood at her side, Olivia's hand linked through his bent arm. Taryn glanced over to her grandmother, then blinked hard, startled by the woman she saw. This was not the indomitable and ageless dictator she remembered, the woman who had been intent on making her life misera-

ble. This was an old woman, her still beautiful face lined
with age, her tall, thin body almost frail.

Taryn had never truly regretted a moment of her life
until now. As she watched her grandmother, she rued all
the years that had slipped away, all the times that she could
have told Olivia that she was frightened or lonely, or that
she just needed a hug. But instead, she had kept her feelings bottled up inside and had punished her grandmother
for the pain it had caused.

She stepped out of the foyer long enough to catch Josh's
eye. He nodded to her, then excused himself from Olivia's
side and headed in her direction. Taryn stepped back into
the shadows and waited. She wasn't ready for this. Not in
the midst of all these strangers. How would Olivia react?
How would she react?

Josh found her, standing next to a huge potted palm, her
hands clenched at her sides, her eyes hidden beneath her
hat brim.

"Hi," he said softly. He bent down to brush a kiss across
her mouth then stroked her cheek with his palm. "I was
wondering if you'd changed your mind."

"I—I think I have," Taryn said. "Josh, I don't know that
this is the time or the place for Olivia and me to work out
our differences."

Josh smiled and kissed her again, this time more deeply.
"Sweetheart, I think it's the best time and place. This is an
important moment in Olivia's life. I think she might be
pleased that you've come to offer your encouragement."

"You didn't tell her I was coming, did you?"

He shook his head. "I didn't want to disappoint her in
case you changed your mind."

Taryn give him a facetious smile. "You didn't want to
send her into cardiac arrest is more like it."

He placed his hands on her upper arms and rubbed gently, then drew her into his embrace. "Taryn, I'm not going to force you to do this. If you want to leave, go ahead."

"Really?"

"Yes. But this will happen soon. You and your grandmother will talk. And then, we'll tell her about us."

"Us," Taryn repeated, savoring the sound of the word as she pressed her face into his crisp, white shirt and crinkled her nose. He smelled like starch and after-shave.

Strange how all her doubts about him had begun to fade since they'd made love. The more he talked about a future, the more she wanted to believe they might be able to work out their differences. After all, he wasn't coercing her into a confrontation with her grandmother. He was making an effort to be more flexible, to understand her wants and needs.

"Olivia and I will talk," Taryn said. "I promise. Soon. But not right now." She glanced up at him. "You're not disappointed, are you?"

"No, never," Josh replied. He flipped his finger down over the brim of her hat in a teasing gesture. "Now, I better get back to Olivia before she comes looking for me and finds you standing in her foyer. Drive carefully on the way home and I'll call you later this evening."

Taryn nodded and kissed him on the cheek, then watched as Josh made his way back to her grandmother. She had been right about him from the very moment they met. There was an inner strength in him that seemed to radiate to those around him. She felt safe and secure in Josh's arms. Maybe she could spend her life with him.

Taryn took one final look at Josh as he placed Olivia's hand back on his arm. Olivia smiled up at him. And then, as if her grandmother sensed she was being watched, she looked in Taryn's direction. Their eyes met for an instant, but there was no recognition there. Olivia's attention was drawn away as another guest stepped into her line of sight.

If her grandmother looked again, Taryn didn't see it. She hurried to the door, determined to make a quick exit. But as she grasped the doorknob in her hand, she stopped. The first step had been taken, why not take the next? What *was* the next step? What would she say, how would she begin?

Overcome by confusion, Taryn turned from the door and headed back to the living room, then stopped dead, changed direction and hurried down the hall. She would just find a quiet place and take a moment to gather her resolve. She opened the first door she came to and froze in the doorway. Years dissolved before her eyes and she was swept back in time to the first day she had arrived at her grandmother's house, a terrified nine-year-old dressed in funeral black. This had been her room.

Pink gingham hung over the windows and decorated the canopy bed that day. The gingham was still there, faded and yellowed now. Possessions of her childhood lined the shelves, toys and mementos that she'd long forgotten, brought home over summer vacation and left there when she returned to boarding school. All she had left of her youth was contained in this room.

Why had her grandmother kept the room as it was? Had she hoped that someday Taryn might return to reclaim her childhood? Taryn smiled wistfully as she picked up a teddy bear from the bed. "Mr. Boonie," she murmured. "No, wait, it's Mr. Boomer, isn't it? So, what have you been doing with yourself all these years?" She held the bear up to her ear. "Just laying around? No wonder you've got a little pot belly. Not enough exercise for you."

"Excuse me." A voice from long ago spoke, now just behind her, standing in the doorway of the room and Taryn stiffened. "The party is going on in the other room. May I ask what you're doing in here?"

Taryn turned, Mr. Boomer clutched in her arms, and slowly removed her hat. Her grandmother's stern look gradually gave way to shock. "Hello, Olivia. I was just visiting with some old friends."

Her grandmother trembled slightly. Taryn watched as she slowly contained her shock and marshaled her defenses. Guilt stabbed through her as she realized Olivia expected an argument. Taryn could see it in her eyes. "For a moment there, I was sure I must have been mistaken," Olivia said. "My vision isn't as sharp as it used to be. But it is you."

Taryn nodded. "It's me. I wasn't sure you'd recognize me." She paused then smiled. "But, I guess you've seen my photos in the papers, haven't you?"

"Why are you here?" Olivia asked.

"Josh suggested I come."

Olivia took a deep breath and fixed a patronizing expression on her face. "I can see you really don't want to be here," she said, her voice quavering slightly. "I don't know what Josh did to convince you to come, but it wasn't necessary. There's no need to put on a false front. Most people know we aren't on speaking terms."

"Well, we are now, Olivia," Taryn replied. "We're speaking and I think, for once, we should try to get along. I'm willing, if you are."

Startled by Taryn's offer, Olivia raised her hand to pat at her hair distractedly. "All right, Taryn. I'm also willing, if you are."

A long silence grew between them as they both stood in the pink gingham bedroom, watching each other uneasily. An eerie feeling of déjà vu hung in the air and Taryn remembered the times they'd stood at opposite sides of this very room, locked in a battle between adolescent and adult.

Now that they'd agreed to start talking, Taryn didn't have a clue as to what to say. It didn't seem to be the time for apologies. Recriminations or accusations would do no good. Maybe congratulations were in order. "Josh told me about your nomination for an Academy Award," she began. "You must be very excited."

Olivia nodded curtly. "I understand that you're to have a gallery showing of your paintings."

"Yes," Taryn replied. "At the Talbot Gallery in mid-April."

Another silence dragged on between them. Taryn decided to push on. "I guess those stories and photos in the tabloids didn't harm your chances too much. I'm glad I didn't spoil things for you."

"I haven't won the award yet," Olivia said. She hesitated. "I saw the photo of you and Joshua in the *Inquisitor*. You seemed to be . . . enjoying yourself."

The last was said with more than a hint of admonishment. "Photos don't always tell the whole story," Taryn said evenly.

"No, I guess they don't." Olivia forced a tight smile. "I didn't think when I asked Josh to seduce you that he'd actually take my request to heart. I just—"

"What?" Taryn interrupted.

"I was just saying that when I made the silly suggestion that Josh seduce you to gain your cooperation, I didn't think he'd take me seriously. When I saw the photo, I—"

"You asked Josh to seduce me?" Taryn fought with a maelstrom of emotions, trying to keep anger and hurt from coloring her voice.

Olivia forced a light laugh. "You were proving to be quite troublesome, Taryn. I thought if he occupied your time with other things . . ."

"Like getting me into the sack?" Taryn shot back.

"There's no need to be vulgar about it," Olivia replied. "Besides, he flatly refused. Josh is a very principled man."

Grabbing Mr. Boomer by the ear, Taryn shoved him under her arm and headed toward the door. "I have to leave now, Olivia. I have some errands to run and a lot of work to do. Good luck with the award and I hope you and Josh get everything you've been hoping for."

Taryn stalked out of the room, not waiting for a reply from her grandmother. To avoid the crowded living area, she made her way through the busy caterers in the kitchen and flung the back door open. It took her a moment to gain her bearings, but then she headed toward the street and her car, tunneling her way through a privet hedge, traversing a rose garden and scaling a fence. As a restless teenager, she'd done all three quite nimbly, after her midnight escapes from her bedroom window. She didn't do quite as well as an adult.

Hurrying toward the street, Taryn pulled the leaves out of her hair and rubbed at the scratches on her arms. Mr. Boomer hadn't fared much better with twigs caught in his fur and his left front paw twisted at a painful angle. She tossed the bear into the passenger seat of the convertible where he landed on his head, then yanked open her car door and slid into the driver's side.

Her hands shook and her heart pounded in her chest. She didn't know whether to scream in anger or burst into tears. Olivia's words repeated in her mind with every aching throb in her temple. Had everything she'd shared with Josh simply been part of a larger scheme? Had he been so focused on securing Olivia her precious nomination that he'd *seduced* her, out of obligation to her grand-mother?

No! She refused to believe his feelings for her were a fraud. He was different. Unlike all the others, he cared about her, he truly did. She could see it in the way he looked at her, could feel it in the way he touched her. She couldn't have been wrong. Those others she had called friends simply wanted something from her. Josh *did* care about her.

But as she silently repeated this assurance, she couldn't allay the doubt that crept into her subconscious mind. Like a scratched record, the tune had replayed itself again and again over the course of her life. Didn't Josh want something from her, too? Isn't that how the whole thing started between them? He wanted her to leave L.A., he wanted her to behave, he wanted her to make peace with Olivia. But out of her element in Los Angeles, her defenses down, she'd let herself be fooled.

Face it, how could Josh, a button-down, straight-arrow tax accountant, possibly love her? What would he want with a spoiled, impetuous party girl like Taryn Wilde? She had no job, very little money, even less education and a wicked reputation in the press—not exactly the kind of girl Josh Banks was ready to take home to mother. Not the kind of woman to be content with a quiet, suburban existence.

And what about her own needs for that matter? How could *she* possibly love *him*? He was rigid and controlling, and entirely unwilling to allow her the freedom to be her own person. She'd suffocate living his well-ordered life-style, always maintaining the proper appearance for the neighbors and the business associates.

Taryn smiled bitterly as she pushed the key into the ignition and started the car. Strange, how the stark realities of life seemed to fade beside the intense, blinding fire of passion. She'd never bothered to objectively examine what waited for them outside the bedroom. And now that she had, she realized that maybe they never truly had a future anyway. She couldn't live in Josh's world, and he wouldn't live in hers.

And love, though a very worthy notion, could not conquer all—at least not for Taryn Wilde.

"SHE'S GONE."

Josh braced his elbows on his desk and pushed his glasses up to rub his tired eyes. He hadn't slept well the past three nights, not since Taryn went missing. Irritated and impatient, he was snapping at everyone, including Olivia.

"Maybe she went back to Europe where she belongs," Olivia suggested. "After all, isn't that what we've wanted all along?"

He looked up at her and scowled. "She doesn't belong in Europe. She belongs here, with me."

Olivia straightened in her chair, adjusting to her most regal bearing. "With you?" she said, arching an aristocratic brow. "Just what is that supposed to mean?"

He'd gone over every word he'd said to her, trying to evaluate Taryn's reactions, her expressions, but he was nearly certain that he hadn't said anything to send her running. Had she simply contracted a bad case of cold feet? Could she regret their night together? "Did she say anything to you before she left your party?"

"Not that I remember," Olivia replied. "We were just talking. What do you mean, she belongs here with you?"

Josh ignored Olivia's question, continuing to dissect everything that happened since he'd left Taryn's bed. "I talked to her friend, Margaux Fortier, but if she knows where Taryn is, she's not saying. She can't go far, she's got a gallery showing in another couple of months."

"Why are you so desperate to find her? I'd think you'd be happy to see her leave. Your life can get back to normal now. You don't have to baby-sit her and I don't have to worry about my award."

"I don't want a normal life," Josh said, aggravated by Olivia's casual attitude toward the woman he loved. "I want a life with Taryn."

Both of Olivia's brows shot up this time. "You . . . and Taryn?"

"I'm in love with your granddaughter," Josh admitted. He hadn't meant to say it so bluntly, but now that the words were out, he didn't really care. It was exactly how he felt and he wasn't afraid to say it.

Olivia laughed. "Josh, you do have a way of alleviating the gloomiest moments. But your sense of humor has taken a terrible turn toward the absurd."

His sense of humor? He shook his head in disbelief. Now he was actually able to make someone laugh when he *wasn't* trying to be funny. He was better off when he didn't have a sense of humor at all. "I'm serious, Olivia. This isn't a joke."

"Don't be ridiculous." Olivia brushed off his words with a wave of her hand. "How could you possibly be in love with my granddaughter? She's wild and unmanageable. You're . . . well, you know how you are."

"She's changed," Josh replied, "and I've changed and even if she hadn't, it wouldn't make a difference to me. I'd love her anyway."

Olivia clucked her tongue and wagged a finger at him. "Joshua, Joshua, Joshua, where is your head? Taryn can be very charming when she puts her mind to it, but she can also be manipulative. She always finds a way to get what she wants. And she's obviously addled your brain doing it. It's just a silly infatuation. You'll get over it soon enough."

"It's more than an infatuation." He paused. "Much more."

Olivia studied him through shrewd eyes. "What do you mean, much more?" Realization began to dawn in her eyes. "Are you saying that you and my granddaughter..." Two spots of color appeared on Olivia's cheeks. Josh wasn't sure they were borne of embarrassment or anger. He decided to take his chances with embarrassment. After all the trouble Taryn had caused her grandmother, sleeping with Olivia's tax accountant would probably be considered a minor offense.

"We made love," Josh replied.

"Oh, my," Olivia said, breathless with shock. She dropped back into her chair and fanned her face. "You and Taryn...but she's just a child. How could you?" Calmly, Josh reached for the pitcher of water on his desk and poured her a glass, then held it out to her.

"I care about Taryn, Miss Wilde. And she is far from a child, she's a woman. A woman I love very much."

"Oh, my." This time, Olivia's words came out as a moan. "My, oh, my."

"And I plan to marry her," Josh concluded.

Olivia immediately stopped fanning herself and snapped her gaze to his. "Marry her? Is that what you said?" She sat up in her chair. "You'd actually make her your wife? Are you sure that's wise, Josh?"

Josh stood and began to pace his office. "That's why it's so important that I find her. Now, do you have any idea what happened? Did you say something to upset her?"

Olivia's gaze darted between his questioning eyes and the glass in her hands. "Well . . . in light of what you just told me, I may have said something."

"What?" Josh demanded, bending over her chair and placing his hands on the arms. "Please, Olivia, tell me."

She shifted uneasily in her chair. "I may have let it slip that I suggested you seduce her to gain her cooperation. At the time, I didn't know you'd gone ahead with my request."

Josh pushed away from her chair and cursed silently. "I didn't seduce her. I mean, not intentionally. It just happened and it had nothing to do with your award, believe me."

"Well, I guess she drew her own conclusions. In addition to being hardheaded, Taryn can also be quite quick to judge. I'm sorry, Josh. It's not that I meant to hurt her. I was just making . . . conversation. I'll apologize to her, as soon as you find her. I promise, I'll set her straight."

"*If* I find her." Josh slowly lowered himself into his chair. "I've had my buddy, Tru Hallihan, checking on some leads, but she's just disappeared. I don't know where else to look."

The buzzer rang on his intercom and Josh reached over and pushed the speaker button. He'd asked his secretary not to disturb him, unless it was word about Taryn. "What is it, Delores?"

"Mr. Banks, there's a package out here that was just delivered by messenger. It's from a Mr. Tru Hallihan. I thought it might be important."

"Bring it in, please." Josh was there to meet her at the door. He grabbed the manila envelope from her hands and tore it open, then withdrew the latest issue of the *Inquisitor*. A note in Tru's scrawl was clipped to the top corner of the front page. "See page 25. Call me if you want me to continue the search."

Josh flipped to the page indicated and skimmed over the layout. His eyes came to a stop at a small picture on the bottom of the page. "Wilde Thing Dumps Tax Accountant for Former Lover."

His heart stopped in his chest. He blinked hard, adjusted his glasses and read the headline again. He had read it right the first time. He moved to the caption. "International party girl and wild thing Taryn Wilde has dumped L.A. tax accountant Josh Banks and returned to Europe with playboy lover Bertrand-Remy Ducharme. The very cozy pair were spotted at New York's JFK, boarding an Air France jet destined for Paris. Sorry, Banks, but it takes a real man to tame a tiger like Taryn. Ciao, Miss Wilde! We'll miss you!"

He stared at the photo. Ducharme blocked all view of Taryn except for a hand and both her legs. For once, he'd done a decent job of protecting her and he'd managed to spirit her right out of the country just as he had promised.

"Dammit, I don't believe this," Josh said. "She's actually left, and with that goofball Ducharme of all people." He'd credited Taryn for having a little more sense than to run away with some spoiled, egotistical idiot. Sure, the guy might be handsome and charming and glamorous, but he was a certified flake.

Had he misjudged Taryn's feelings for him *that* badly? So, maybe she had been angry about Olivia's inopportune comment, but Taryn got angry about as often as the sun rose and set in the sky. She usually chose to dig in her heels and fight, not run and hide. Certainly, she must have known how he really felt about her, what their lovemaking meant to him.

"May I see that?" Olivia asked.

Josh tossed the newspaper across his desk. "She's gone back to Europe."

Olivia glanced down at the paper, then looked back up at Josh, concern filling her expression. "Don't you find this ironic?" she said with a laugh. "We've spent the last month trying to get rid of her and now that she's obliged us, we suddenly want her back. What are you going to do?"

Josh leaned back in his chair and stared at the ceiling of his office. "I don't know that there's much that I can do," Josh murmured.

"Balderdash," Olivia said.

Josh glanced over at her. "What?"

"You heard what I said. Quit moping around and feeling sorry for yourself. My granddaughter is a smart girl. She'll realize her mistake and she'll be back. You'll just have to be patient."

"What if you're wrong?"

Olivia pursed her lips and gave him a long-suffering look. "Joshua, she has a gallery opening in another two months. She's got to come back for that. And when she does, you'll just have to convince her to forget this Bertrand person and stay in the States."

Josh pushed out of his chair and rubbed his eyes again. "I've got to get out of here. I haven't slept in days and I can't think straight. Come on. I'll walk you out."

"Everything will be all right, Joshua," Olivia assured. "I promise."

By the time Josh reached Bachelor Arms he was almost dead on his feet. His head ached, his legs were like dead weight, and he could barely see through his bloodshot eyes. Pulling the front door open, he stopped and stared over at the brass plaque. "Believe the legend," he muttered.

As he made his way to his apartment, he passed 1-G and noticed the door was wide open. "I'm not going in there," he murmured. "That mirror is to blame for this whole damn mess." But his curiosity overwhelmed his common sense and he stepped inside. The apartment was empty, except for a few boxes and the mirror. He slowly crossed the room, then stood in front of the ornate frame and stared at his reflection. Geez, he looked like hell.

"Hey there, Josh."

Josh spun around. Tru stood in the doorway, a box in his hand. When he caught sight of Josh, his brow furrowed in concern. "Geez, you look like hell."

"I know," Josh said. "What are you doing here?"

"Amberson found someone to rent this place. He gave me twenty-four hours to clear out the rest of my stuff or he'd sell it all. Hey, did you get the package I sent?"

Josh rubbed the back of his neck, trying to ease some of the tension. "Yeah, I got it."

"So, do you want me to track her down in Europe?"

He shook his head. "No. She'll have to come back for her gallery opening soon . . . I think."

Tru walked over to the small kitchen area and began to fill a box with the contents of a drawer. "You're in love with her, aren't you?" Tru said.

"The guy is gonzo. Head over heels." Garrett stood in the doorway, his hands braced on either side of the doorjamb. "Geez, Josh, you look like hell."

"So I've been told," Josh said.

Garrett stepped into the apartment. "You finally moving out, Tru?"

"Yep. Caroline's at home right now picking through the first load of boxes. She claims she's taking a scientific look at the trappings of bachelorhood. I think she's just hoping to find out more about my previous girlfriends."

"What previous girlfriends?" Garrett asked.

"My point exactly," Tru replied. "But she doesn't believe me." Tru shook his head and chuckled. "Women."

"Women," Josh echoed, a bitter edge to his voice.

Garrett grinned lasciviously. "Ah, yes. Women. Well, at least there's one of us left to maintain the reputation of this building."

"You think so?" Josh asked. "Just take a look in that mirror."

"No way," Garrett said.

"You mean you believe in all that garbage about the ghost?" Tru challenged.

"Better safe than sorry," Garrett replied.

"Some woman probably made the whole thing up just to scare all the bachelors in this place," Tru teased. "Right Josh?"

Josh nodded. "Tru's right. I guess it worked, too. Look at you, trembling in your loafers."

Garrett wagged his finger at Josh. "I liked you a lot better when you didn't talk so much. Taryn Wilde has been a bad influence on you."

"Maybe so," Josh said. He walked over to the mirror and looked into it. "Look here. I don't see anything."

Tru joined him at the mirror. "Me neither," he said.

"What, you think I'm scared?" With a confident swagger, Garrett joined them. The trio stared at their reflection for a long moment. "I guess you're right," Garrett said.

Tru turned and started toward the door. "I'm finished here. You guys want to stop at Flynn's for a beer?"

Josh glanced over his shoulder. "I'll stop for one," he said. He looked over at Garrett. "What about you, McCabe?"

Wide-eyed, Garrett stared into the mirror, not blinking, not moving. "Do you see that?" he whispered, reaching out to touch the glass.

"What?" Josh asked.

"There, in the mirror."

Josh followed Garrett's outstretched arm, but all he saw was two reflections, his and McCabe's. He slapped Garrett on the shoulder. "Quit kidding around, McCabe. Come on, let's go."

Josh joined Tru at the door, but Garrett still hadn't moved. "You think he's seen her?" Josh asked beneath his breath.

"I'd say chances are pretty good," Tru replied.

"Then heaven help him," Josh said. "'Cause he's in for the ride of his life."

"ARE YOU SURE you will be all right here on your own, Taryn?"

Taryn glanced around the spacious hillside house, then nodded to Margaux. "It's beautiful. A perfect place for an artist to work." It was a lovely home, airy and filled with sunlight, with huge windows and French doors overlooking an exotic garden. But what Taryn didn't say was that she had her doubts whether she could work *anywhere* right now.

She'd fled Olivia's party with no particular destination in mind and she'd ended up in Palm Springs. Carrying no luggage, Taryn had checked into a room at an expensive spa and spent the next four days eating her way through the junk food in the minibar and watching all the pay movies on television. The management had finally asked her to leave when her credit card went over the limit on smoked almonds and fifteen-dollar-a-can goose liver *pâté*.

She'd decided to call Margaux to request a short-term loan, but instead the gallery owner convinced Taryn to come back to Los Angeles. Margaux had good cause to regret her insistence that Taryn return. Taryn had called off the gallery opening at least once every hour since then and had threatened to return to Europe on the half hour. After only one morning of coddling her newest artist, Margaux, in a fit of French pique, packed Taryn's clothes, her supplies, and her canvases and hustled her off to picturesque Santa Barbara.

"This house belongs to a sculptor friend of mine," Margaux continued. "He is spending a few months in Europe and then he has a showing in New York. There is a lovely studio on the upper floor. All your supplies and canvases are up there."

Taryn walked over to the open French doors and stared out at the lush garden from the terrace. The scent of bougainvillaea drifted on the breeze and the sound of the wind in the eucalyptus and the palms soothed her nerves. Somewhere in the distance a Mariachi band played. On the horizon, the Pacific glittered beneath the noonday sun. She drew in a deep breath and, for an instant, the salty tang of the ocean air cleared her hazy mind.

"The pace here is different, Taryn. Less frantic. I believe you might find it easier to work. And this whole community is filled with artists and galleries. You will feel right at home."

Taryn looked out over the lovely Spanish-style houses of the city. Strangely enough, she did feel at home here. The whitewashed walls and red tile roofs of the houses, the thick greenery and exotic flowers, reminded her of the small villages that dotted the Costa del Sol, where sundrenched Spain curved to meet the blue of the Mediterranean Sea.

"Maybe you're right, Margaux. Maybe I will be able to work here."

The gallery owner stepped to her side and shot her a sideways glance. "Would you like to tell me what happened between you and your accountant?"

"Nothing that I shouldn't have expected," Taryn replied offhandedly. "I just suffered from a momentary malfunction of my bastard radar. For a few weeks, I was completely blind to every fraud and user on the planet, including Josh Banks."

"Then it is over between you two?"

Taryn smiled ruefully. "It never really started."

"He came looking for you," Margaux offered.

Taryn's head snapped around and she stared at Margaux in disbelief. "What?"

"A few days ago. Of course, I did not tell him where you were. At that time I did not know you were pigging out on overpriced junk food in Palm Springs. He seemed concerned."

"The only person Josh Banks is concerned about is the great Olivia Wilde."

"So you don't want him to know where you are?"

"I suppose he'll find out sooner or later. Unless I stay holed up in this house twenty-four hours a day, the tabloids will show up here in a few days. It's like I leave a little trail of bread crumbs for the vultures. They always find me."

"Not this time," Margaux replied. "I think you have made your last appearance in the scandal sheets. For a while, at least."

"What are you talking about?"

Margaux grabbed her bag from the couch and withdrew a crumpled sheet of newsprint. "The latest issue of the *Inquisitor*, page twenty-five. It hit the newsstands this morning."

Taryn glanced down at the headline over the photo. "'Wilde Thing Dumps Tax Accountant for Former Lover'?" she read. She squinted at the two figures in the picture. The male was instantly recognizable—Berti. With JFK International as the backdrop, Berti held up his jacket to protect his companion from the camera lens. All Taryn could see of Officer Julie Knowles was one arm and two feet. "That's not me. That's Berti and his policewoman. How could anyone mistake her for me? She's got to be at least six feet tall. And look at those feet! They're huge."

"Don't question good fortune, darling," Margaux replied. "As far as the tabloids and the rest of the world are concerned, you have left the country."

A tiny smile twisted the corners of Taryn's lips. "I've left the country," she repeated. "That's what he wanted all along. Well, I guess he and Olivia will be happy now."

"And what about you, darling? Will you be happy?"

Taryn stared out at the ocean. "I don't know, Margaux," she replied. "Some day, if I'm lucky, maybe I'll forget what I felt for Josh."

It was easy to say the words. But Taryn knew they wouldn't come true anytime soon.

9

THE WESTERN HORIZON was alive with color—fiery orange, brilliant pink, dusky purple. Taryn sat on the weathered wood bench, her feet tucked under her and her arms crossed over her knees. The Santa Barbara sunset had become a regular habit with her over the past month. She'd rise with the sun in the morning and paint in the light-flooded second floor studio until late afternoon. Then, she'd stroll through the streets of the picturesque neighborhoods in search of the perfect view for the next sunset.

For a time, she'd walk up Anacapa Street and watch from the top of the county courthouse's clock tower. The building stood sentinel over the lovely city, its towers and turret, lacy ironwork and colorful tile, rivaling some of the most luxurious palaces Taryn had visited in Spain. She would watch the setting sun gleaming off the terra-cotta roofs of the homes before it turned their white stucco walls a pale pink.

But as the days grew longer, she had wandered in the other direction on Anacapa Street, to the wharf, where she sat at the end of the pier and watched as night officially began. Now, in the dusky twilight, she walked home, carrying a paper bag filled with dinner from her favorite deli. The schedule never changed. In a few hours, after a dinner of tuna salad on whole wheat and chicken noodle soup, she would methodically clean her brushes and plan the next day's work. Then she'd crawl, exhausted, into bed.

For two weeks after her arrival in Santa Barbara, she had moped around the house, cursing Josh Banks and her own gullibility, trying to bury her feelings for him. Then one morning, she awoke at sunrise and felt compelled to paint. Now, a month later, she obsessed about maintaining an exact schedule, fearing that if she altered it in any way, the creative wave she was riding would suddenly dissolve beneath her feet and thoughts of Josh Banks would return to haunt her.

She couldn't allow herself the time to regret what had happened with Josh. Instead, she tucked the memories of their time together in a distant corner of her heart. Someday, when she had the strength and the confidence, she would take them out and deal with them one by one. But for now, she focused all her energies on her painting and tried not to think about her return to Los Angeles—to the place where Josh Banks would be near enough to touch.

Her mind flashed back to their night together, to the incredible passion he aroused in her, to the sweet contentment she'd found as she'd slept in his arms. She cursed inwardly and pushed his image from her mind. The gallery opening was just two weeks away and she couldn't afford to let those kinds of thoughts back into her mind. In her mind, at this moment, Josh was Everyman. He had ceased to be the man she loved.

Taryn pulled the house keys from the pocket of her sundress and fumbled to unlock the front door. When the lock stuck, she clamped the bag between her teeth and wiggled the key until the bolt slipped.

"Hello, Taryn."

She jumped, startled by the voice, then spun around to come face-to-face with her grandmother. The bag dropped to the ground with a soft thud. Taryn stared down as her dinner came to rest on one of her grandmother's designer pumps. Chicken noodle soup slowly seeped onto the expensive leather.

Olivia lifted her foot and gave it a little shake, trying to dislodge a noodle. When the effort proved unsuccessful, she simply ignored her shoeful of soup with an imperturbable facade.

"How did you find me?" Taryn asked.

"It wasn't easy," she replied. "I finally got hold of that balmy Frenchman of yours. He told me that despite tabloid reports to the contrary, you hadn't returned to Europe with him. Then I stopped by the gallery and had a little talk with your friend, Margaux Fortier. She told me where I could find you."

"Why are you here?"

"Where are your manners, young lady? The proper thing to do is invite me inside," Olivia said.

"I've never claimed to be proper," Taryn said.

"Nevertheless, we have certain sensitive subjects to discuss and I'd rather that we don't air our family laundry on the street for everyone to see—and hear."

Taryn pushed the front door open. "All right, Olivia." She led her grandmother to the living room and motioned for her to sit on the couch. Taryn took a chair directly across from her. "Say what you've come to say."

Her grandmother straightened her spine and folded her hands in her lap. "I'm sorry," she said, her words simple and direct.

Taryn blinked in surprise. These were the last words she ever expected to emerge from her grandmother's mouth and she was completely unprepared to reply.

"I made a mistake," Olivia continued.

"Which mistake are we talking about, Olivia?"

"Don't be impertinent, Taryn. You know what mistake I'm talking about. That statement I made about you and Josh Banks."

Taryn nodded slowly. "Oh. You mean that thing about him seducing me. Well, Olivia, you'll be pleased to know that *wasn't* a mistake." She paused. "Funny, you don't look surprised."

"Joshua told me that you two had . . . had . . ."

"Done the wild thing?"

Two spots of color appeared on Olivia's pale, wrinkled cheeks. "Been intimate. I believe that's the polite way to put it. But he told me that he didn't . . . do it because I asked him to. I believe he was acting on his own accord."

"Is that what he told you?"

"No," Olivia said. "Not exactly."

Taryn smiled cynically. "What were his exact words? Tell me, I'd like to know."

"I believe he said 'I love your granddaughter, Miss Wilde.' He said more, but by that time I was feeling a bit faint and I really wasn't listening any longer."

Taryn stared at Olivia, dumbfounded. "You expect me to believe that?"

"Of course. I'm telling you the truth. The poor boy seems to genuinely love you. He's been off his mark ever since you left Los Angeles. He believes you returned to Europe with that French . . . what was it he called him? Flake."

Taryn frowned and gnawed on her lower lip. This couldn't be true. Josh, in *love* with her? Olivia must have misunderstood. Taryn Wilde was the last person in the world Josh Banks would choose to love.

"I think it would be best if you came back to Los Angeles. It's my fault that you left and now I want to put things right. Before Joshua completely loses his mind, and all my money right along with it."

"I—I can't go back," Taryn said. "Not now."

"But why not? Don't you believe what I've told you?"

"I'm not sure. But if I leave here, I . . . I just can't. I have a lot of work to do before my showing."

"Do you love him, Taryn?" Olivia asked.

"I don't know," Taryn said softly. "Maybe."

"But you will talk to him when you get back, won't you?"

"I don't think we have anything to talk about, Olivia."

"Taryn, I care about Josh. He has been very good to me and I don't want to see him hurt."

"Why? What is he to you? He's just your business manager."

"He's more than that," Olivia said, her eyes downcast. "There was a time when I was desperate and I went to him for help. I had spent nearly all my money, I hadn't worked in over ten years, and the bills were beginning to pile up."

"But you were retired."

"That's only what I told people when they asked. I was too ashamed to admit that I hadn't had a decent offer in ages. Nobody wanted me."

"But the money, all that tuition for the boarding schools, the clothes. I know it didn't come out of my trust fund. Where did it come from? Olivia, tell me. How did you pay for it all?"

"I spent my savings. All of it was gone. But then Josh gave me a second chance for a secure life. The nomination has given me a second chance at a career. And now I'm asking you to give me just one more chance to be a grandmother to you."

Taryn twisted her fingers in her lap. She'd never realized what her grandmother had sacrificed. "I—I don't know. It's been so long."

"Whether you want to believe it or not, I care about you," Olivia said. "You're my granddaughter and the only thing I have left of my son. You're stubborn and reckless and incredibly talented. You're exactly like I was when I was your age."

Taryn smiled tentatively. "I've always suspected I had too much Wilde blood running through my veins."

"Taryn, come back to Los Angeles with me. My driver is waiting outside. We can pack your things right now. You can attend the award ceremony with me tomorrow night. And then you can talk to Josh and straighten out this mess that I've caused."

"I can't," Taryn cried. "I have to stay here and finish what I've started. If Josh really does care about me, he'll understand and he'll wait. Have you told him where I am?"

"Not yet," Olivia replied.

"Then I don't want you to tell him. I'll deal with Josh when I return to Los Angeles. I need these next few weeks to sort this all through."

Olivia nodded, then stood and smoothed the skirt of her designer suit. "All right, if that's what you want, I won't try to convince you otherwise."

Taryn walked Olivia to the door. "Thank you for coming. I'm glad we had this little talk."

Olivia hesitantly reached out and squeezed her granddaughter's hand. "Josh is a good man. And it would be nice to have him as part of our family."

Taryn smiled. "I'm not going to marry Josh for you," she said. "I've done a lot of crazy things to gain your approval, but I'll only go so far and I stop long before life-long commitment and fidelity."

"Well, maybe you could marry him because *you* want to," Olivia said.

"I'm not even sure if he *wants* to marry me. We've got to figure out a way to get along first," Taryn replied. "And I'm not about to tackle that problem until after my opening."

Olivia gave her hand a squeeze. "I'd like to come and see your paintings."

"I'll call Margaux and have her send you an invitation. And bring all your friends. I'm going to need the support."

"I will. Now, I must be going. I have a lot to do before tomorrow night." Her grandmother strode down the sidewalk toward the car with a brisk step.

"Good luck with the award, Olivia," Taryn called.

Olivia turned. "Not good luck!" she cried dramatically. "You're a member of one of Hollywood's greatest families, Taryn. It's 'break a leg!'"

THE TALBOT GALLERY was ablaze with light and sound. A string quartet played Mozart as guests drank champagne and nibbled on hors d'oeuvres. But the art took center stage, each painting hung and lit to its best advantage.

Taryn watched the crowd from the second floor gallery, her hands clutching the steel railing. Margaux stood below, guests gathered around her, preparing for the introduction of her newest discovery. Taryn descended the steps to polite applause like a princess greeting her courtiers, her serene smile hiding a bad case of the jitters, her floor-length dress hiding her knocking knees.

From that moment on, she schmoozed—charming the critics, discussing her work with important collectors and making small talk with the rest of the guests. Faces blurred together and introductions went in one ear and out the other. Her face became stiff from the constant smiling and her mind rattled with every word she'd babbled that evening.

After an hour of chatter, Taryn rubbed her aching temples and decided to take a break. As she excused herself and made her way to Margaux's office, the room suddenly became silent. All eyes turned toward the door and a buzz of whispered exclamations rippled through the gallery.

Olivia Wilde stood regally in the doorway, the queen mother coming to pay a visit to her princess. The room broke into applause and Olivia nodded, graciously accepting the crowd's congratulations for her recent Academy Award. A surge of pride overcame Taryn and she smiled as she watched her grandmother make her way into the gallery. A fresh start, a new lease, a promising future. They'd both reached the same place in their lives and now they'd continue on, together as a family.

Taryn slowly crossed the room, the crowd parting as she approached Olivia. "Hello, Grandmother. I'm glad you could come."

Olivia reached out and gathered Taryn's hands in hers. "I wouldn't have missed your special night for the world. Now, I want you to give me a private tour of your brilliant work."

Taryn tucked her grandmother's hand in the crook of her arm. "I'd be happy to."

As they wandered through the gallery, Olivia tipped her head toward Taryn's. "I spoke to Joshua today," she whispered. "I tried to convince him to accompany me here, but he refused. He still believes you've thrown him over for that Frenchman."

"You didn't tell him the truth?" Taryn asked.

Olivia smiled. "I got in enough trouble the last time I put myself between you and Josh."

"It's better that he doesn't come," Taryn said. "I don't think I'm ready to talk to him yet."

"And why not? Now that you understand this was all just a silly misunderstanding, you should try to patch things up. After all, you're in love with him, aren't you?"

"Grandmother, there's more to this than just a misunderstanding. Josh and I are so different. I'm not sure that we could ever be happy together."

"Balderdash," Olivia replied. "I refuse to believe that you two can't work out your problems."

"I don't want to talk about it right now," Taryn said. "Now, what do you think about these paintings?"

Olivia frowned in frustration then turned to look at the newest Taryn Wilde series. Her eyes grew wide and her gaze darted among the three canvases. "Oh my," she breathed. "Why, that's . . ."

"What do you think?" Taryn asked, a hopeful catch in her voice.

"I think . . ." Olivia paused and took a steadying breath. "I think they're very . . . sensual. Beautiful. Stirring. There's a—a silent strength about these paintings that's very . . . breathtaking."

Taryn smiled. "I'm glad you like them." A flood of satisfaction coursed through her and she realized how important her grandmother's approval was to her.

"In fact, I love them," Olivia said, slipping her hand around Taryn's waist and giving her a hug. "Now, you better get back to your guests. I've monopolized enough of your time already."

"You'll be all right by yourself?"

"Taryn, I've been mingling with the best of them for years. My public awaits."

Taryn watched as her grandmother worked the crowd, smiling and accepting congratulations for her recent success. Drawing a deep breath, she turned toward Margaux's office. But then a familiar figure appeared in the doorway and she froze. Her heart fluttered in her chest and her pulse began to race.

He looked different, tired and a bit thinner. His soft brown hair, usually neatly trimmed and combed, now brushed the starched collar of his crisp, white shirt. Taryn closed her eyes, willing the image to disappear, but when she opened them, he was still there, his gaze skimming over the crowd.

Taryn stepped behind a panel, then slowly worked her way through the maze of temporary walls until she reached Margaux's office. She slipped inside and shut the door behind her. But she was alone for only a few moments before the door crashed open.

"He is here!" Margaux cried, her white-knuckled hand clutching the doorknob.

"I know," Taryn said. She disengaged Margaux's fingers from the door and shut it behind her. "When I saw him my heart started racing and I couldn't breathe. I've been hiding out here, trying to calm down and figure out what to do."

"I do not blame you. He does not look happy," Margaux said. "You know, you are going to have to talk to him."

Taryn nodded. "I know, I know. I guess there's no way to avoid it, huh?"

"It would be considered a snub if you didn't."

"All right," Taryn said, trying to inject a note of determination into her voice. "If you think that's best."

"Darling, I know what I speak of. Trust me."

Taryn's hands drifted to her hair. "How do I look? Is my hair all right? What about this dress? Maybe I should have worn something more . . . conservative."

"Do not worry how you look. It makes no difference to the beast. He is blind to things such as this." Margaux turned and peered out the door. "*Zut*. He looks like he is constipated," she commented critically.

"What?"

"Constipated. I believe the word is the same in English, *non?* You know, when . . ."

"I know what the word means, Margaux."

She stepped aside. "Here. Take a look. See for yourself."

Taryn peered out the door. "Oh, my God," she gasped. "That's Edwin St. Andrews."

"Of course. Who did you think I was talking about?"

"Josh," Taryn said.

"Josh? That tax accountant you have been sulking about. He is here?"

"That's who I thought you were talking about."

"*Mon Dieu*, he is the one who smashed the canvas over St. Andrews's head." Margaux groaned and collapsed against the wall. "They will see each other and it will be all over. I have never had a brawl in my gallery. Until now. My reputation will be destroyed."

"You won't have a brawl," Taryn said. "I'll keep Edwin occupied while you keep Josh busy. Give him a tour of the gallery, show him the storeroom. Just keep him away from Edwin. The Executioner will only stay long enough to put his stamp of disapproval on my work. That should take about five minutes." Taryn drew a shaky breath and pulled the door open. "Wish me luck. I feel like I'm jumping into a pool full of sharks."

Taryn stepped out of the storeroom and slowly approached the critic. He stood before her new series, his brow furrowed, his index finger tapping against his downturned lips. She wiped her damp palms against her skirt, then thrust out her hand.

"Good evening, Mr. St. Andrews," she said.

Edwin looked down at her hand with a distasteful expression, as if she were holding out a dead fish for him to touch. "Miss Wilde."

"I—I didn't expect you to come."

"This is an opening—I'm a critic. It's my job," Edwin said.

"But, I just thought that after . . . after that unfortunate incident, you wouldn't—"

"Miss Wilde, I am here. Now, be quiet so I can concentrate and do my job."

Taryn winced and bit her lower lip. "Would you like me to discuss any of my work?"

"Just stand there, silently, if you must," he ordered. "If I have any questions, I'll ask."

Taryn dutifully remained at the critic's side, staring at her paintings as he completed his evaluation, her knees shaking and her hands trembling. She felt as if her life hung in the balance, as if a simple word or two might change everything. But as she watched the critic evaluate her paintings, her thoughts continually drifted in another direction, to another man that waited and watched, somewhere in the gallery.

Sooner or later, she'd have to face him, too.

"HELLO, TARYN."

Josh watched as Taryn stiffened slightly, but she refused to turn around and face him. Instead, she ignored his greeting and resumed her conversation with Edwin.

"I—I did this piece while I was living in Barcelona. I was inspired by the bull fights and the matadors, the color and the pageantry against the backdrop of such danger and violence."

He spoke again, this time more firmly. "Taryn, you can't avoid me all evening. We are going to talk."

Slowly, she faced him. Their eyes met and for a single, shattering moment his breath stopped in his chest. Lord, she was beautiful. His blood warmed and he was tempted to pull her into his arms and kiss her, to melt the ice from her eyes and the frozen expression from her lovely face.

Taryn swallowed hard and forced a smile. "Hello, Josh," she murmured. "It was . . . nice of you to come."

As Edwin turned beside her, Taryn's gaze suddenly turned frantic, bouncing between Josh and Edwin, waiting for the first punch to be thrown. But Josh merely smiled at the critic and held out his hand. "Edwin, glad you could make it tonight."

"Good to see you again, Josh," Edwin replied.

Taryn gawked at them both.

"What do you think of Taryn's show?"

"I'll hold my comments for my column," Edwin said. "Now, I must be going." He took Taryn's hand. "Miss Wilde, congratulations. A very. . . interesting exhibition. Very interesting, indeed."

Taryn's gaze followed the critic as he walked through the crowd and out the door.

Josh glanced around the gallery. "Where's Berti?" he asked.

Her shoulders slumped and she moaned softly. "You've done it again," she murmured. "I was talking to Edwin and he actually seemed to be . . ." she searched for the appropriate word. ". . . interested. He seemed to be *interested* in my work."

"I thought for sure he'd be here," Josh continued. "After all, this is your opening. What kind of man is he that he'd miss your big night?"

"You've chased him off," Taryn cried.

"Berti?" Josh asked.

Taryn spun around to face him. "No, Edwin St. Andrews. You've done it again."

"Done what?" Josh asked.

She glared at him, her hands now clenched at her sides. "Ruined everything," Taryn cried.

He'd forgotten how her eyes sparkled when she was angry. "Taryn, where is Berti? Isn't he here?"

"No! He's not, and I wish you'd stayed away, too."

A surge of relief washed over him. So, Taryn had left the Frenchman in Europe, exactly where he belonged. Without Ducharme hanging around, Josh stood a good chance of getting Taryn to listen to reason. They belonged together and he wasn't about to stop at anything less than total commitment.

"You don't have to worry about Edwin," Josh said, following her despondent gaze to the doorway of the gallery. "I took care of him."

"You took care of him? What is that supposed to mean? Did you threaten him again?" She cursed beneath her breath.

"I didn't threaten him," he said. "Edwin and I had a little talk and we made a deal."

"You made a deal, using *my* career as collateral?" Her voice rose and several of the guests turned to stare.

"I stopped by the *Post* the day after the television show," Josh explained. "We talked and we came to an agreement. He said he'd give you a fair shot and I agreed to do his taxes. He says you're good. Still, he won't give you anything more than a mediocre review. I guess he doesn't give better. It was the best I could do, so take it or leave it."

"Edwin St. Andrews said I was good?" Taryn said, her voice suddenly breathless.

"His exact words were, 'She has a rather intense, though somewhat unfocused, passion.'" Josh mimicked the critic to perfection, right down to the haughty look in his eyes.

"I thought that's what *you* said," Taryn returned.

"He was talking about your painting," Josh replied. His hands circled her waist. "I was talking about something else."

Taryn watched him with ill-disguised suspicion. "You think this will make everything all right between us?"

"I thought it might help," Josh said.

She pulled out of his grasp, then slapped at his hands when he tried to grab her again. "Well, think again. This just proves my point. You're not happy unless you're supervising my life, are you?"

Josh finally got hold of her elbow. "Come on. I'm not ready to have this discussion in front of all your guests."

"I'm not coming with you," she said, yanking her arm away. "If you want to talk to me, you can wait until the evening is over, until I've done everything I can to salvage my career. If that's not good enough for you, tough."

"All right," Josh said. "I can wait. But don't think you're going to leave here tonight without talking to me, Taryn." Her gave her a meaningful stare, a look that told her he wasn't kidding. Then he turned and walked away, his silent command still hanging in the air. He'd let her wait for now, but by the end of the evening, she'd be ready to talk.

They circled the gallery all night, watching warily, never coming within twenty feet of each other. The tension between them was nearly unbearable and he had to stop himself from dragging her into a dark corner and kissing her senseless. Every now and then he'd catch her staring at him from across the room, their eyes connecting, and a crackling current of electricity seemed to shake them both. It was as if an unseen power kept pulling them closer by degrees, until, when the room had finally cleared, they stood just a few feet from each other.

As Taryn stood next to Olivia at the door, he decided to make his move. Josh stepped up to her and grabbed her hand. "Olivia, you'll excuse us, won't you? Taryn and I have a few things to discuss."

Olivia gave him an encouraging smile. "It's about time, young man." She leaned over and kissed Taryn on the cheek. "Don't let him bully you, my dear." Then she turned to Josh and kissed him on his cheek. "And don't you let her get away." She smiled warmly at them both, then turned and walked toward the door.

"Come on," Josh said. "It's time we settle this once and for all." He dragged her toward the storeroom at the back of the gallery. Once inside, he shut the door behind them.

Taryn snatched her hand away. "Of all the overbearing, arrogant—"

He reached up and cupped her face in his palms, then covered her mouth with his. The words died in her throat. The kiss was long and deep, melting her resolve so thoroughly he felt her go weak in his arms. His blood heated as she moaned beneath his lips and he grew hard with long repressed desire.

"I've missed you, Taryn," he murmured, his mouth soft against hers.

"I haven't missed you," she murmured, still consumed by the kiss. "It's been very nice to run my own life for awhile."

"I haven't tried to run your life, Taryn," he said. "I just want you to be happy and I'm willing to do what it takes to make that happen." He kissed her again, this time trailing his lips along her jawline to the soft hollow beneath her ear. He sucked gently on her perfumed neck.

"What about Edwin?" she asked, tipping her head to the side and arching her neck in a silent request for more.

"I was just fixing a big mistake I made. What about Berti?"

Taryn shifted in his arms, then pressed her hands against his chest and pushed away from him. She shook her head as if clearing away the haze of passion that seemed to envelop them both. She smiled ruefully. "Berti's in Europe. He got married last week to that policewoman he met at the Beverly Hills jail. I never went back to Europe with him."

Josh grinned. "Then there's nothing to stop us from starting again?"

She looked at him, her pale eyes wide and questioning. "Can we, Josh? We're so different in so many ways. Maybe we're just not meant to be together."

"I don't believe that," he said, his voice firm, uncompromising. "And neither do you."

She sighed. "Don't you tell me what I believe and what I don't believe!" Taryn said stubbornly. "This is exactly what I mean! You're always trying to bully me into thinking the narrow-minded way you think. Well, I'm not going to do it, Josh Banks. You can just—"

With a growl of frustration, Josh bent over and grabbed Taryn around the legs, then tossed her over his shoulder. He opened the storeroom door and stalked out into the nearly empty gallery. There was only one way to deal with this obstinate, fiery, beautiful woman he loved.

"Put me down!" she shrieked, her voice echoing off the high ceilings and the polished wood floor.

"Forget it. I'm not going to put you down," Josh replied, heading toward the door. "If I have to go through the rest of my life with you tossed over my shoulder, I will. Dammit, I love you, Taryn. Like I've never loved another human being in my entire life. And I will do anything to keep you with me."

Taryn pushed herself up, bracing her arms on his back. She twisted in his arms and craned her neck to see his face, but he refused to look at her.

"Stop!" she shouted.

He did as she asked.

Her voice came softly from behind him. "You love me?"

"Yes," he replied, staring straight ahead. "And I want to marry you. Will you marry me, Taryn Wilde?"

A giggle, the most musical sound in the universe, drifted up through the silent gallery. "This is not the way it's supposed to go," she said. He could hear the mischievous smile in her voice. "You're supposed to get down on bended knee and stare soulfully into my eyes as you ask me that question. Right now, we're just staring at each other's backsides. It's not very romantic."

"Well, Taryn, you and I are going to rewrite the book on how things are supposed to go. And this is my proposal, so take it or leave it. Will you marry me?"

The room went silent and he held his breath.

"Yes," Taryn whispered, her arms snaking around his waist from behind. "Yes, I will marry you, Josh Banks. And yes, I do love you." She gave him an upside down hug and then kicked her feet in childish delight.

Josh slowly let go of his tightly held breath. She said yes. Taryn Wilde had agreed to marry him. *Yes.* A single word that would change his life forever. A low, deep chuckle began in his throat then burst from his lips. For a moment, he wondered if he might be slipping into some unexplained hysteria, but then he swallowed hard and tried to stop laughing. He had to be crazy, that was the only explanation. He was actually going to marry Taryn Wilde!

"Stop laughing and put me down," she demanded. "I want to kiss you."

Josh started for the door. "Not yet."

"Josh, come on," she protested. "Put me down."

He pushed open the door to the gallery.

"Wait, wait, wait," Taryn cried. "We can't leave yet. I have something to show you."

"Taryn, this is not the time for games."

"No games," she said. "I swear."

"All right, make it quick," Josh growled. "We've got a long drive ahead of us."

"Over there," she ordered.

He glanced over his shoulder, then followed her directions, weaving through the gallery. She stopped him in the center of the huge room in front of a wide partition that held three paintings, the bullfight series that she had been discussing with Edwin St. Andrews.

"Put me down," Taryn demanded.

"No," Josh replied.

"I promise, I'm not going anywhere. Now, put me down, I have a surprise for you."

Josh lowered her to her feet and watched as she straightened her disheveled dress. He kissed her once, long and hard, then grabbed her by the hand for safety's sake, not trusting that this was just a ruse. If he was smart, he'd never let go. The thought of ever losing Taryn was too much to bear.

"Cover your eyes," she teased.

"Taryn, I'm not that stupid. And I'm a lot faster than you, believe me."

"All right," she conceded. "I'll cover them for you." She stepped behind him and placed her palms over his eyes. He had to bend his knees for her to reach and he held on to her wrists to keep track of where she was. Gently, she steered him around the partition, to the paintings on the other side. Then she pulled her hands away.

"Ta da!" she sang. "What do you think?"

Josh stared at the paintings. He had glanced at them before, but he hadn't really studied them. The series pictured a nude male, asleep amidst a tangle of sheets. He stepped closer and looked at the small tag beside the middle painting.

Joshua: Number Two.

"This is me?" Josh asked, his voice soft with disbelief.

"Do you like them?" Taryn asked.

He smiled and nodded slowly. "Yes . . . I do. They're incredible. But when? I didn't pose for these. I was sitting on a stool. With my underwear on."

She shrugged. "That night, after you fell asleep, I got up and made some sketches. Margaux says they're my best work. She's sold all three to major collectors and she wants me to do another series."

He looked at her, then back at the paintings. "And everyone here tonight has been staring at these paintings . . . of me . . . with my clothes off . . . naked . . . nude?"

She wrapped her arms around his neck and smiled contentedly. "Don't worry. The paintings may be good, but they don't come close to the real thing."

"The real thing?" Josh asked incredulously.

"Yes," she murmured. Pushing up on her tiptoes, she brushed a kiss across his lips. "I'm the only one who gets to see the real thing from now on."

IN THE EARLY MORNING hours, they made love again and Taryn explored his body like a true artist, bringing him to peaks of pleasure that he'd never known existed. When they were both sated, Josh rolled to his side and kissed her softly. She untangled her leg from the twisted sheets and slid it up over his hip.

"Are you happy?" he whispered.

"Blissfully so," Taryn said as she stretched against him, molding her soft body to his.

"You don't think we've been reckless? Impetuous?"

She slowly dragged her foot down the length of his bare leg. "To a fault," she purred. "But what else could we do?"

Josh drew his thumb along her lower lip. "I promise we'll take a proper honeymoon. We'll start planning it as soon as we get back to Los Angeles. Where would you like to go? London, Paris, Rome?"

Taryn grinned mischievously. "Forget proper. I've been to London and the food's terrible. Paris smells funny if the wind is from the wrong direction. And Rome has way too many pigeons for my taste." She looked around the room. "I kind of like this place. Al's Honeymoon Haven. Mirrors on the ceiling, a bathtub for two, and a heart-shaped bed. The best that Las Vegas has to offer."

Josh drew his finger along the length of her perfect nose. "You know, Olivia's going to blow a gasket when she finds out we got married in a round-the-clock wedding chapel by an Elvis impersonator," he said.

Taryn shrugged. "Then we'll get married in a proper church ceremony and we'll let her plan the entire thing. Will that make you happy?"

Josh laughed. "Forget proper, Taryn Wilde Banks. I don't think I'll ever be happy with proper again."

Taryn slipped her arms around his neck and kissed him playfully. "No, my darling husband, I don't think you will."

* * * * *

Next month, don't miss *A Happily Unmarried Man* (April 1995, #533), Kate Hoffmann's third and final delightfully funny book for Temptation's exciting Bachelor Arms miniseries. Discover how determined bachelor Garrett McCabe gets an unwanted lesson in domestic bliss from homemaking expert Emily Taylor.

What happens when three best friends from college reunite years later for a wedding . . . especially when the bride has cold feet? JoAnn Ross will captivate you with her sexy and intriguing stories: *Never a Bride!* (May 1995, #537), *For Richer or Poorer* (June 1995, #541) and *Three Grooms and a Wedding* (July 1995, #545).

Soon to move into Bachelor Arms are the heroes and heroines in books by bestselling authors Candace Schuler and Judith Arnold. Don't miss their stories!

HARLEQUIN®

Temptation

Secret Fantasies

Do you have a secret fantasy?

Carol Glendower does. More than anything, she
wants her husband back. Evan was handsome,
sexy…perfect. But he's gone, and she's alone.
Carol will have to risk *everything* to fulfill her
fantasy. Dare she?

Find out in #534 THE TEMPTING by Lisa Harris,
available in April 1995.

Everybody has a secret fantasy. And you'll find
them all in Temptation's exciting new yearlong
miniseries, Secret Fantasies. Beginning January
1995, one book each month focuses on the hero
or heroine's innermost romantic fantasy.…

MILLION DOLLAR SWEEPSTAKES (III)

No purchase necessary. To enter, follow the directions published. Method of entry may vary. For eligibility, entries must be received no later than March 31, 1996. No liability is assumed for printing errors, lost, late or misdirected entries. Odds of winning are determined by the number of eligible entries distributed and received. Prizewinners will be determined no later than June 30, 1996.

Sweepstakes open to residents of the U.S. (except Puerto Rico), Canada, Europe and Taiwan who are 18 years of age or older. All applicable laws and regulations apply. Sweepstakes offer void wherever prohibited by law. Values of all prizes are in U.S. currency. This sweepstakes is presented by Torstar Corp., its subsidiaries and affiliates, in conjunction with book, merchandise and/or product offerings. For a copy of the Official Rules send a self-addressed, stamped envelope (WA residents need not affix return postage) to: MILLION DOLLAR SWEEPSTAKES (III) Rules, P.O. Box 4573, Blair, NE 68009, USA.

EXTRA BONUS PRIZE DRAWING

No purchase necessary. The Extra Bonus Prize will be awarded in a random drawing to be conducted no later than 5/30/96 from among all entries received. To qualify, entries must be received by 3/31/96 and comply with published directions. Drawing open to residents of the U.S. (except Puerto Rico), Canada, Europe and Taiwan who are 18 years of age or older. All applicable laws and regulations apply; offer void wherever prohibited by law. Odds of winning are dependent upon number of eligibile entries received. Prize is valued in U.S. currency. The offer is presented by Torstar Corp., its subsidiaries and affiliates in conjunction with book, merchandise and/or product offering. For a copy of the Official Rules governing this sweepstakes, send a self-addressed, stamped envelope (WA residents need not affix return postage) to: Extra Bonus Prize Drawing Rules, P.O. Box 4590, Blair, NE 68009, USA.

SWP-H395

HARLEQUIN®

PRESENTS
RELUCTANT BRIDEGROOMS

Two beautiful brides, two unforgettable romances...
two men running for their lives....

My Lady Love, by Paula Marshall, introduces
Charles, Viscount Halstead, who lost his memory
and found himself employed as a stableboy by the
untouchable Nell Tallboys, Countess Malplaquet.
But Nell didn't consider Charles untouchable—
not at all!

Darling Amazon, by Sylvia Andrew, is the story of
a spurious engagement between Julia Marchant
and Hugo, marquess of Rostherne—an engagement
that gets out of hand and just may lead Hugo to
the altar after all!

Enjoy two madcap Regency weddings this May,
wherever Harlequin books are sold.

REG5

Harlequin invites you to the most
romantic wedding of the season.

Rope the cowboy of your dreams in
Marry Me, Cowboy!

A collection of 4 brand-new stories,
celebrating weddings, written by:

New York Times bestselling author

JANET DAILEY

and favorite authors

Margaret Way
Anne McAllister
Susan Fox

Be sure not to miss Marry Me, Cowboy!
coming this April

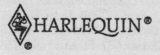 HARLEQUIN®

MMC

BACHELOR ARMS SURVEY

Vote for Your Favorite!

If all these guys were bachelors, who would you most want to catch? Please! Just choose one from this delectable dozen!

1 □ Mel Gibson
2 □ Sean Connery
3 □ Kevin Costner
4 □ Alec Baldwin
5 □ Denzel Washington
6 □ Tom Cruise
7 □ Andre Agassi
8 □ Michael Jordan
9 □ Jack Nicholson
10 □ Robert Redford
11 □ Paul Newman
12 □ Keanu Reeves

We want to hear from you, so please send in your response to:

> In the U.S.: BACHELOR ARMS,
> P.O. Box 9076, Buffalo, NY 14269-9076
> In Canada: BACHELOR ARMS,
> P.O. Box 637, Ft. Erie, ON L2A 5X3

Name: _____

Address _____ City: _____

State/Prov.: _____ Zip/Postal Code: _____